Death of a Seer
Book 1
of The Seer Series
By
Alisha B. Davis

Acknowledgements

To my family, thank you for always supporting me and listening to this story over and over again for the past 10 years. To my children, I love you. DJ, remember who you are -- a king. Pud, I am so very proud of you; thanks for being my push. Last but not at all least, my pastors Vince and Ashley Thomas, thank you for the time you spent praying for and speaking into me. I love you and The Outlet Community Church family.

About the Author

Alisha Davis was born the third of four girls to her parents, Garland and Marietta Davis. She is the mother of two: a son, Terrel, and a daughter, Ceara. In 2005, she was diagnosed with Lupus SLE, a very destructive autoimmune disease. The disease progressed to lupus nephritis in 2007, damaging her kidneys to the point that she was not expected to live. However, as she tells it, God had promised her too many things for her to die, and she refused to accept the prognoses. Some say she is lucky to have escaped death numerous times, including a run-in with a tractor-trailer, in which her car landed underneath it. She does not call it luck at all, however, but instead calls it God's favor. At a very early age, she began to see in the spiritual realm. She sought out anyone to explain more about the angelic and demonic beings she saw, but she found out that she was one of only a few. This fictional story has elements of her life and experiences within the spiritual realm.

Chapter 1

She felt the cold air and a bumping that jarred her body.

"Oh," Bertha moaned. She tried to clear her mind; she could not seem to open her eyes. All she heard were unfamiliar voices. When she finally managed to pry her eyelids open, she saw a Latino man in a uniform standing beside her. She shook away the remaining fogginess. Where was she, and who was this man? The last thing she remembered was being in the grocery store before she was to meet Estella for their weekly lunch. She felt cold air, then two more bumps. She blinked and tried to clear her mind. Her eyes were very heavy, so she kept them closed for a while and then heard more unfamiliar voices. She struggled and finally managed to open her eyes again.

What happened, and why was she lying down? As hard as she tried, she could not recall what had happened to her at the store. As she pondered her current state, she realized that she was being pushed and that she was cold. She felt the air on her chest. Lifting her head, she discovered, to her horror, that her bra had been cut into two pieces down the middle, and her breasts were exposed. Flushing with embarrassment, she tried to reach to cover herself and discovered she was strapped down.

Realizing his patient was awake; the young EMT announced in a heavily accented voice, "You're okay."

As he pushed her through the double doors, a strong antiseptic smell assaulted Bertha's nose, letting her know she was in a hospital. She knew the smell all too well with her many visits over the past few years.

Trying to make sense of it all, she turned to the young woman who had now taken the Latino man's place.

"What happened to me?"

Her voice was more of a whisper that no one heard.

From her gurney, Bertha watched as fluorescent lights and the occasional head and shoulders of someone moving out of the way of "Team Bertha" went by. It seemed that the plump-faced blonde standing beside her now was in charge.

She looked down at Bertha and, seeing she was awake, yelled, "She's conscious! Can we get some more fluids over here?"

Bertha looked at the name badge clipped to her pocket; it read Mitzi. Mitzi proceeded to barrage Bertha with a battery of questions.

"Do you know your name?"

"Bertha Henderson." Bertha struggled to get up.

"What year is it?"

"2012."

"Who is the President?"

"Obama."

"What day is it?"

"Tuesday." Slightly annoyed and still a little hoarse, Bertha asked, "Where am I and why am I here?"

"You're at Emory Hospital. You passed out at the grocery store, and you were brought here."

Without so much as a breath, Mitzi continued, "Do you have any medical conditions we should know about?"

"I have Lupus."

Immediately, Bertha repented to herself for saying that. She never wanted to take ownership of the disease that had ravaged her body for the last seven years. She always answered with "I was diagnosed with Lupus," but now clearly was not the time to debate the matter. There were more pressing issues like speaking to Estella. She had to be wondering why she had not picked her up or called, Bertha thought, as she spotted a clock that read way past the time of their scheduled lunch date. Her mind turned to Savannah. She could envision the concern on the face of her only child. She knew that if she did not call at least once a week, Savannah would be concerned. She had intended to make the call later when she knew they would be home and her grand baby was still up.

If she missed the call, Savannah would be worried and start calling, first Bertha's cell then her home number, repeatedly. How that girl became such a worrier was beyond comprehension, Bertha thought. She quickly censored her thoughts. Savannah had good reason to worry. Although they were close, Savannah lived in Las Vegas and would not be able to "get to you in a hurry" as she would so often tell her mother. So, in an effort to ease Savannah's anxiety, Bertha came to visit a few times a year. Between visits, there were weekly calls. Bertha looked forward to speaking to her grand baby, Dominick. He was the love of her life.

There was no telling what Savannah would do if she did not get the call, not to mention Dominick, who got to talk on the phone all by himself. Bertha continued to dwell on her daughter. Savannah would worry once she found out. Bertha remembered the concern she had on her face the last time they were together. Where was her cell phone, purse, and her car? Bertha dreaded letting anyone know what happened, but she was in a pickle. How was she going to get back home, she wondered?

A smile touched her lips as Bertha thought about how blessed she really was. She had plenty of loved ones and friends. She thought about her late husband of twenty-three years, Solomon, now gone for the last five. He had been there with her through it all. Thinking about him reminded her of how upset he would get when she was sick. Good thing he was not here to see this, she thought. He could fix anything that broke around the house. It was strange how he would get mad because he could not fix her. Remembering him was like a deep breath of cool air; it felt good. Savannah was another matter altogether. She constantly begged her mother to move to Las Vegas so that she could keep an eye on her. "No," Bertha would always say jokingly, "But you can send my grandbaby to live with me!" It became the ritual saying that would break up the seriousness of the moment.

After her dad's passing, Savannah was careful to listen for any sign that her mother may need her. Although Savannah was in Las Vegas, she knew by the sound of Bertha's voice if she was alright. By far, the best medicine in the world was Dominick. So when she heard something that did not sound quite right, she would let Dominick talk extra long. He would sing his favorite songs and tell Bertha all about preschool, his teachers, and friends. That little boy was her heart, and after talking to him she always sounded better.

Bertha pictured his little, round, chocolate, dimpled cheeks smiling at his Nannie. That was what he called her. He had tried to say "Granny" and it came out "Nannie." That is what she would forever be, his Nannie! She had spoken to him last week, promising to send him something special. She pictured him asking everyday if the box was here yet. For this three-year-old, a day was like a year. Savannah scolded her countless times about spoiling him with so many gifts, but it fell on deaf ears.

"That's my grandchild and I am going to do what I'm going to do," Bertha would say.

Thoughts of her loved ones made her momentarily forget about her current predicament. Then she thought this would be alarming to Savannah, but Stella, (her nickname for Estella) her best friend, was another matter. If she didn't reach her soon, Stella would be calling Savannah. Then everyone would be alarmed.

In a matter of minutes Bertha was wheeled to an area that she could only assume was triage. After being subjected to the usual assault — IV adjustments, blood pressure and temperature — she was stripped of the remains of her clothes. Now properly adorned with the hospital's fashionable open-backed gown, she was wheeled into a regular hospital room.

"Oh shoot," she thought, "I won't be going home today!"

She was going to have to make the call. Now to get someone to get her cell phone. While waiting for a nurse to respond to the buzzer, she looked around, dreading yet another hospital stay. She had never liked hospitals. She hated their sterile smell and surroundings, the constant prodding and poking. She was never able to sleep well. And then there were the vampires — her name for the people constantly sticking her for countless vials of blood. Having spent so much time in them over the past five years, she positively hated them! However, she was thankful to be at Emory this time. It was here that she first got the dreaded diagnosis.

As hospitals go, she felt that Emory was the best in the Atlanta metropolitan area. More than once she had recommended the hospital to one of her ailing friends. Despite it being a teaching hospital, the staff seemed to concern themselves with a high level of courtesy and consideration for each patient. As a patient, you had to be subjected to at least two, possibly three, sets of attending physicians and their students, but even the young doctors seem to have a congenial manner while getting educated by your afflicted body.

After introducing himself as the emergency room physician, Dr. Campbell, a tall dark-skinned black man, said, "We need to take some tests."

"Tests for what?", Bertha asked. Dr. Campbell turned over the pages on the clipboard he held. After seeing the furrowed brows of this strikingly handsome man, Bertha asked, "What's wrong?"

"We'll know more after the test results come back."

He gave her a weak reassuring smile and left the room. A moment later, Mitzi returned with all the tools she would need to take yet more vials of blood. At the sight of them, Bertha rolled her eyes and sighed.

Mitzi joked, "I'll be sure to leave you some."

Making quick work of her duties, she left with seven vials. She turned and stuck her head back in the door and asked, "Oh yeah, who is your primary care physician?," she asked.

Bertha gave her the information and she was gone again. Alone now, the thoughts she had been trying to push to the back of her mind slowly took over. She knew that she must have had a flare up. She had not felt very well all week and it was raining really hard. The rain always made the pain in her joints excruciating. This morning she took her usual dose of two Tramadol and two Tylenol just to take the edge off the pain.

She was always in pain, but what happened differently today?" she wondered. This time, she had passed out. She hadn't done that in a long time. In agony, with every joint of her body aching and her back on fire, Bertha began to pray. Her mind now racing, she stopped; she needed to call Estella first.

"What am I going to do? How can I get out of here without a big fuss? There was no way to avoid it now," she thought.

"I won't call anyone until I know when they will let me out," she said to herself. "Father," she managed through the pain, "I am so tired and just want to be healed from all of this. I know You are able, but I have prayed this prayer so many times only to be right here once again. I don't understand why You won't heal my body. I really don't know how You are getting the glory out of my life in this state. It just seems unnecessary, and I am mad at You."

Listening to herself, she had to chuckle just a bit because she sounded like Savannah as a young girl when she did not like a punishment that had been handed down.

Bertha heard that still small voice that was so familiar to her say, "It is never My will for you to suffer. I want you always to be in health and prosper. I am your God and My word never fails."

"But I don't understand why I am still sick, and here I am once again in the hospital." She queried the air.

"I healed you on the cross. You choose to accept the diagnosis rather than My Word. When you were told that you had Lupus, you accepted it and took it as your own. You only went part of the way by saying you were 'diagnosed,' rather than saying you 'have Lupus.' You believed the test results rather than My Word. When you walk in only part of the promise, you will receive only that part. But I am the Lord your God and I meet you where you are. Your complete healing was always there for you to accept, but you did not believe. So, I used you in this illness to help you see My grace in your life and to be a witness for others. You encouraged people wherever you went. That was your purpose here. The doctors, nurses, patients, and staff that you encountered were changed by the words you spoke. Even though you were not walking in complete healing, you spoke faith that I was able to heal."

Bertha wanted to argue, but she knew it was useless. With those words, the morphine dripping into her veins began to work, and Bertha closed her eyes.

Chapter 2

For a moment, there was only darkness, still and quiet. It surrounded her and she felt like giving into it. She thought about just melting away into the darkness. She was tired, in pain, confused, and did not want to endure any of it any longer. The word from God should have made a difference, but she was still in agony. What was she doing all of this praying for if she still had to suffer? She should have given up a long time ago.

"What has serving God ever gotten you?" The voice, sounding like her own whispered now in her ear. "You need to just turn away from God and die. He is not even real. You have wasted your life serving a non-existent God with nothing to show for it."

The voice was about to go on when all of a sudden a piercing bright light shone. Bertha squinted against the brightness. There was something in the light, something familiar. Yes, it was her longtime companion, Marcus.

"It's you," she thought, as he put his finger to her mouth to quiet her thoughts, although she had not made an audible sound. Bertha began to watch Marcus as he left her

side suddenly and moved in front of her. He stood rebuking the other. Yes, it was the other one. She gave a slight shiver as she watched their exchange.

Marcus was her guardian angel sent to protect Bertha while she was still in the womb.

"This one is special. I have much for her to do," God had told him before he was sent to earth to protect the unborn child.

The Master never fully told any of His angels the plan for one of His chosen ones' lives, but with His command, there was no need to question. So, with the instruction to protect, he had set about his duties. From conception until now, Marcus had protected Bertha from all kinds of calamities. Before her birth, Bertha should have died when her mother fell and began to hemorrhage. After the emergency C-section was performed and the cord taken from around her neck, she was safe for only a moment. Bertha was one of only two babies that survived dysentery that spread through the Neonatal unit, killing thirteen babies.

When she was a little girl of four years, Marcus started appearing to her in visions. He told her that he was assigned to her for her protection and not to be afraid, because she was special to God. Her little mind did not understand it, but she knew she could trust him. He seemed very tall to her little eyes. His skin was the color of honey, his eyes were brown like her Daddy's, and he had black curly hair. She immediately felt at ease. She looked at him and saw only goodness and the glow of glory that came from being in the presence of God. Yes, this was her friend, Marcus, that she told everyone about.

Bertha was ignorant of the gifts she possessed and the dangers she would face. She thought everyone could see as she could. When she began to talk about Marcus to her parents, they just wrote him off as an imaginary friend that most kids have at that age. It wasn't until later that her mother took notice of the repeated times that her daughter had cheated death. Her mother always joked that if it was going to happen to anyone, it was going to be Bertha. As the years passed, there were many assassination attempts, but she was protected from them. It would become the ongoing family joke that she was a super girl. No one knew why she was apparently invincible. Time and time again, Bertha would come out of an impossible situation completely unscathed.

Later in her life, Marcus was joined by three more angels. Somehow, she instantly knew their names just by looking at them. After Marcus, came Jonas, The Encourager, at the age of fourteen. He was there when she was so down about school and not fitting in. He encouraged her to embrace her differences and that God would use her because she did not fit in with others. Then just two years later, Paul, Spiritual Insight, arrived. It was this angel that helped Bertha to know the world she lived in was just a shadow of the real. He showed her how her world was just for an instant, but the real realm, the one she could not see, was eternity and it was more a reality than she knew. At the age of twenty-four, Bertha came into a boldness that she had not known before. At the time, her walk with God was not what it once was although she knew the truth. Marcus, Jonas, and Paul were then joined by Fred, Speak the Truth. He prompted her to be more aggressive with regard to her faith and anyone who challenged it.

Presently, Bertha did not see any of the other angels. She could only see Marcus. She could hear Marcus call the demon, Adonis. This was the first time she ever heard him refer to it by name, although she was very familiar with the creature. It had been with her almost as long as Marcus had. His attacks were constant and progressive. While she watched the scene, she thought back on the many car accidents, surgeries, and illnesses that should most certainly have taken her life and remembered she had seen the thing at every one. Yet again, this creature was trying to kill her. "But God!" she said out loud. At that utterance Adonis stumbled, but recovered quickly. Then she heard an audible voice say, "Pray!"

"Your assignment is over," Marcus told Adonis. "You have not won, nor will you." Marcus continued to converse with Adonis and Bertha watched while she prayed.

"Wait a minute," Bertha thought, "the assignment is over, that means...Oh God no," she pondered, then continued to pray, watch and listen.

Adonis said, "I was given the task to kill her or separate her from the Father. I was there at her birth when you protected her from our attack," he said. "We saw what you were doing," Adonis continued. "You surrounded her and the other one in the hospital. Satan assigned me to her, back there outside of the hospital. Finally, I can be rid of her and you," Adonis spat at Marcus! "I could not get her to renounce God, but I did get her to kill her child.I was close," he said.

"Her soul belongs to Jehovah," Marcus retorted. Bertha continued praying while she continued to listen to the two spiritual beings.

Marcus seemed to tower over Adonis although they were nearly the same height. As she prayed, Bertha remembered Adonis from the time she was very young. She could see him looking at her through her bedroom window. The first time she saw him she screamed and cried and called out for her parents to come make the monster go away. Her parents comforted her but wrote off the hysteria as normal childhood behavior. It was Marcus that would let her know that she was safe. Although Adonis could change his shape, his eyes were always the same. They were dark yellow with black centers. There was also the unmistakable smell. She would get a whiff of rotting flesh and knew he was around. It lingered in her memory long after he left. He followed her most of her life and here he was again.

Adonis was one of Lucifer's best and highest-ranking principalities. He had the ability to change from the vile, grotesque creature he was to several different other personae, depending on the situation and who needed to be influenced. He could walk among the humans if he needed to, but it was much easier to use the weak, so they were the tools he relied on the most. When he did not have the authority to do physical harm, he would use weak people in direct contact with his target and influence their behavior against the target. He was relentless in his attempts to convince Bertha to kill herself or, at least, walk away from God. The mission never changed, although throughout the years, the method did.

Adonis almost had Bertha when she was nineteen. he planted the suggestion that she would be better off aborting an unwanted pregnancy. Feeling so ashamed of her situation, she relented to the voice telling her to do this unspeakable act. After she did, he returned to heap guilt and shame on her; he vomited and defecated on her. She spent many years under the weight of her decision. Adonis was able to accomplish this because Bertha believed all that he said and walked away slowly from God. As she did this, her vision of the spiritual realm dimmed. She relied on herself and what she wanted to do. It was not until she ran into an old childhood friend whom God spoke through that she came to her senses and returned to what she knew. Although she repented and knew that God forgave her, she never really forgave herself. This left the door open for Adonis to remain a permanent fixture in her life. He waited patiently and after a while, he would strike again and again, bringing up the incident time and time again in her mind.

One day after dwelling on the aborted baby, Bertha just did not feel right. She had joint pain, but it was never in the same joint for long. After a few months, her husband, Solomon, prompted her to see a doctor. She did not really want to because it wasn't constant and it moved around. Besides all of that she had never been sick and did not have time for it with Savannah in high school. Her days were busy with teaching and taking care of her family. She tried to make her case for why she did not need to see a doctor, but Solomon pulled Savannah into the matter to coax her into obedience. With the two of them joining forces and never letting up, they convinced her. Bertha went to the doctor and got the diagnosis of Lupus. She could finally put a name to what was wrong with her body and so she accepted it as her fate and punishment for what she had done so many years ago. In the back of her mind, she accepted it as the will of God. Although she had been taught differently, the guilt of the abortion stayed with her and it left her open to Adonis.

After family and friends heard the news of the diagnosis, they offered their sympathy and home remedies. Everyone wanted to be the one to cure Bertha with this new product that they happened to be selling. From special water, to exotic fruit juice from the jungle of a distant country, all of this was thrust upon Bertha and she tried it all. If people were not offering her "the cure," they were trying to ascertain why she was sick, what had she done.

The church women were certain that Bertha was having an affair and that is why she was sick. They started the rumor and it spread like wildfire. With the church being mostly single women, they were eager to be the next Mrs. Henderson, so they perpetuated the whole story. Each sister added new juicy details to the story. Adonis danced around like a school child in the church, prancing from one woman to another. This church was his playground; he and thousands of other demons lived in the walls like termites.

One sister approached Solomon directly with a sympathetic touch on the arm and a hot meal she made just for him because she knew he was not being taken care of at home. He, being the man he was, graciously refused and he, Bertha and Savannah left the church promptly. Solomon did not understand why Bertha was so unaffected by all of it. She would always say their fight was not against flesh and blood and that would be the end of it. Although married, she had told him very little about what she saw in the spiritual realm. He loved and trusted her and had learned to rely on her wisdom over the years. Bertha knew that Solomon was "the right one,"the one God had created just for her. They had lived and loved through life's ups and downs.

The thoughts of her life swirled around in her head like a hurricane.

"Pray!" She heard again.

This time she complied quickly and as the words left her lips, Marcus again began to advance on Adonis. After a while she could not think of what to pray so she started quoting scriptures that she memorized. Finally, when she had recited all that her mind could regurgitate, she simply repeated the only thing that she could think of—the name Jesus.

"Mrs. Henderson?"

A voice calling her name brought her back to consciousness. Before her stood yet another doctor. "Mrs. Henderson, my name is Dr. Patel and I am head of the nephrology department of Emory." Bertha studied the man before her. He was not very tall with latte colored skin, black hair with a few gray ones sprinkled throughout. He spoke with a slight accent that she could not identify right away. As she pondered his ethnicity, she realized he was speaking and she needed to pay attention. "Wait, please repeat that," she said. He gave a slight sigh and began again. "The results of the test we took are back. There is no easy way to tell you this. Your kidneys are shutting down and you need a transplant immediately." He paused for a moment then continued. "We checked the national database and there are none available at this time. We will keep looking, but in the meantime we will make you as comfortable as possible."

Bertha listened carefully to the slight accent in the kind tone of this new doctor. She felt for him now as he tried to explain her condition to her. He was compassionate she could tell.

"What about dialysis?" she asked.

"Not possible as a long-term solution. Your kidneys are too far gone. You have only a few days before they completely shut down. Do you have family or a pastor that we can call to be with you?"

"Yes, but what aren't you telling me? Just say it."

"You don't have long to live. We will do everything we can, but barring a transplant or an act of God, there is nothing else we can do."

Mitzi asked," Is there someone I can call for you?"

"Yes, my friend, Estella, and my daughter. If you could get my purse, I will get the phone numbers."

Finding the purse at the base of the bed, Mitzi handed it to her. Retrieving her cell phone, Bertha called out the phone numbers as Mitzi wrote them down. A dull ache seemed to crawl up from Bertha's stomach that was not associated with her pain.

Tears ran down her face and she called out to God, "Is this it? Lord, your word says that You would give me whatever I ask in Your name. I am praying that You heal my body. I am tired of all the pain, drugs, hospitals and all these people. Lord, I just want to be done with all of this, but God, Your will be done."

She cried. Finally succumbing to the pain and drugs, Bertha let sleep come and overtake her. The bright light she saw earlier returned lighting up her hospital room. A heavy mist filled the room. As the mist lifted, two enormous lions walked into the room. They didn't frighten her. In some unknown way, she was comforted by them. The light highlighted their thick manes and fur with a gold sheen. They turned their gaze onto Bertha. In unison they spoke as one.

"Tell everything you have seen. Write it all down. Do it now, for you don't have long."

With those words she was finally at peace. God's will was being done as she said. Bertha awoke as two attendants slid up the sides of her bed and began to roll it out of the room.

"We're moving you to ICU," one of them told her. As the words pressed into her consciousness, Bertha knew the urgency to place everything down on paper. She must leave a record! Once in the new room, Bertha asked for pen and paper before they left. She began the task of relating what God has been showing her all those years to her beautiful daughter, Puddin', her nickname for Savannah.

"God, give me the words," she prayed.

Chapter 3

"Bertha," Estella said, as she snatched up the phone without looking at the caller ID.

She had paced the floor until she was tired. She knew something was wrong, very wrong. Bertha was never late; it was just not like her. If she were going to be late, she would call.

"Mrs. Martinez?" the voice asked.

"Yes," Estella answered, a chill touching her heart.

"Mrs. Henderson asked me to call you. This is Mitzi. I'm a nurse at Emory Hospital. I need to let you know Bertha Henderson is here at the hospital."

"Is she okay?"

"I would suggest that you get here as quickly as you can. She is in room 548."

"What is going on? How is she?"

"She is not doing well at all. You need to get here as quickly as you can."

Replacing the phone, Estella sank to her knees. Tears streamed down her face, streaking her makeup. She felt like someone had punched her in the stomach, knocking all the wind out. Without a thought, she called her grandson to come and pick her up to go to see about her best friend.

"*Abuela*," Raul answered the phone, "What's up? I can't talk right now. I'm at work."

"I need a ride to the hospital," Estella replied.

"Are you okay?" he asked in a panic.

"Yes, I am fine. It is my friend, Bertha. She is sick. They took her to Emory."

"I'm sorry, Abuela, but I can't take you now. I can't until the morning. I am working late today."

"Oh, okay *nieto*. Just come as soon as you can. I will be waiting for you."

"Is Miss Henderson going to be okay?"

"I don't know, but it does not look good. That is why I need to get there as soon as possible."

"Do any of your other friends have cars?"

"No. Bertha was the only one."

Hearing the panic in his grandmother's voice, Raul assured her. "I will come right after I get off, okay?"

"Okay, Raul. Muchas gracias, nieto."

"Okay. Bye, Grandma."

"Hello?" Savannah said, holding her breath.

She recognized the Atlanta area code, but not the number. No one called her cell phone at this time of day unless it was an emergency. Everyone that was close to her knew the conditions on her job. They knew about her supervisor, Robert King, and knew how much of a jerk he was. They wouldn't have put her through anymore trouble unless it was an emergency.

"Is this Miss Henderson?" the female voice asked.

"Yes."Savannah answered. She didn't care that she used her maiden name.

"My name is Mitzi Near, from Emory Hospital. I'm afraid I have some disturbing news. Your mother, Bertha Henderson, is in critical condition and you need to get here as soon as possible."

"Oh God, please!" Savannah whispered, tears coursing down her face.

"I tried your other number and then this one. Please come as soon as you can. It's not good!"

Savannah heard the deep concern in the woman's voice as she gave her the hospital and room number.

"I will leave today," she replied, turning her chair around and seeing her supervisor Robert King staring at her. She looked away. She dialed the number that Mitzi gave to her and was connected to her mother's room. Mr.

King made a motion for her to hang up the phone. Savannah could care less about him right now. The only thing that concerned her now was hearing her mother's voice.

"Lord, please don't take my mother. I need her," she prayed silently.

The phone rang, but there was no answer. Savannah removed her headset and was packing to leave when her phone beeped signaling an incoming call. Looking down, she saw it was Jonathan, her husband.

"Babe, the hospital called..."

"I know", she interrupted. "I just spoke with the nurse." Tears were flowing in a continual stream down her face. "I'm coming home. Can you please book me a flight out?"

"Of course. Are you alright?" Jonathan asked.

"I don't know. I can't lose her, Jonathan. I can't!"

"Come home, honey."

"I'm on my way."

By now a few of her co-workers on the floor knew something was happening and were on their feet looking over their cubicles. Her cubicle mate, Jean, whispered that Mr. King was on his way. Savannah didn't care as she tried calling her mother's room one more time.

Seeing her on the phone again, Mr. King shouted.

"Savannah, I want to see you in my office immediately! Now, if you want to keep your job!"

Finally, she heard her mother's voice. "Mom, it's me! I'm coming! Hang on . . . I'm coming!"

Bertha responded, but Savannah couldn't understand what she was saying since her voice was so garbled.

"Mom, what are you saying? I can't understand you! Mom, Mom!" she shouted but heard nothing.

The phone was dead! Panic took over every fiber of her being. Dropping her cell phone into her purse she began to sign off her workstation phone and pack up.

"I'll do that. You'd better see Mr. King," Jean told her.

Walking toward her supervisor's large corner office, Savannah remembered her first day on this job over four years ago. Excited that she finally had a job that would help pay for school, she had worn her best suit — the navy suit she knew fit her well. The navy pumps accentuated her long slender legs. Her 5'10 frame was highlighted. She had displayed confidence that she really didn't feel. Trying to bring her nervousness under control, she had brushed her long, wavy hair back over her shoulder. It hung down the middle of her back. She hardly ever wore it loose, even though everyone told her how pretty it was. *"But they don't have to deal with it,"* she always thought. The white band she wore to contain it framed her smooth, chocolate brown complexion. She was a beautiful woman. At least that's what many people said, but she didn't feel it. She had her Dad's complexion, but her mother's features. She knew her mom was beautiful, with a small nose, a sparkling smile, and lighter skin. She always wished she looked more like her.

She had sat across from the man that would become her supervisor and finally end those three days of interviewing. Mr. King had raised his head from the pile of supposedly important papers, an act he had adopted to make the person he was interviewing understand how important his time was. Now appraising the newest hire, he had been struck by how beautiful she was. Her rich brown complexion shone with a glow that seemed to come from inside her. Her slender frame made that suit seem tailor-made. Brushing back her hair again, a nervous reaction, Savannah had waited for him to speak. One part of Savannah had been drawn to this ruggedly handsome light-skinned black man. She had seen in his eyes his appraisal of her. That he was interested in her was obvious. Although his manner had been strictly business, his eyes had told another story. He had risen from his seat and moved to the front of his desk diagonal to Savannah. When he stood she had realized that he was just shy of six feet tall and a little over 200 pounds, which he carried on a very muscular frame. She could tell he worked out. As handsome as he may be, Savannah was very cautious about any relationships with lighter skinned black men first, and men she worked with second. They often acted as though she should be grateful for their attention because of her darker skin. She was keenly aware of colorism in dealing with white people, but even more so within her own race. Thinking about it had made her go on guard. She was proud of who she was. Her mother had made sure to remind her of the greatness that lay within. Despite all her mother's encouragement, she still knew that lighter skin was better than dark in the world she lived in. Everything told her that she was not as good because she was milk chocolate colored.

"Ah, Miss Henderson, why do you think you'll be an asset to this company?" Mr. King had asked her after introducing himself, his eyes searching hers.

"Because I will bring my abilities and willingness to take on any task. My reliability has been proven by my past jobs." she said. "May I ask you a question?"

"Sure. What is it?"

"Is this another interview? I was informed I had the job. Is that not true?"

"Oh yes, yes you have the job, but you will be working under me and I need to know your character for myself," he said moving back to his chair behind the desk. "*This one will have to be watched*," he thought.

After giving Savannah her schedule and showing her to her cubicle, Mr. King had escorted her to the security office for her badge and keys. When she had glanced in the glass of one of the offices along the way, she had caught him looking at her butt.

That was how she had started four years ago. Robert had asked Savannah out several times since that time. The one time she had gone out with him she called her mother to get her opinion of him. "*Mom always knows who people really are*," she thought.

Bertha instantly told her to stay away from him. "Going out with your boss is a big mistake," she said. Savannah took Bertha's advice and since that rejection, he has made her life at the job hell, finding fault with anything to do with her.

Before Robert could say anything Savannah told him about her mother. She was crying and not really making the words come out clearly.

She said, "I have to go see her."

Mr. King said nothing and then looked at his computer. "You have a week of vacation time remaining for the year." Sarcastically he continued, "I can only allow you a week off." Savannah cried and yelled. "My mother is dying!"

"I hope she gets better in five days!"

"You bastard!" Savannah yelled as she left slamming the door and knocking off some framed awards on Robert's wall.

All eyes were on Savannah when she returned to her desk.

Speaking to Jean, she said, "My mother is in the hospital. I have to go see her." She grabbed her things and started again to straighten her desk.

"Savannah, just go home. I will take care of all this."

As she was leaving, Mr. King yelled after her, "Remember, you only have a week."

Savannah yelled back, "Just shut the fuck up!"

Now the whole floor was standing and staring at Savannah and Robert. There were several audible gasps and whispers. Everyone knew that Savannah never swore. She was considered one of the nicest people there. However, they also knew that, for some reason, Robert had it in for her. He was constantly belittling her and pointing out any mistakes in front of the team. When he felt she was at the point of quitting, he would ease up and give her a little praise. He reveled in his seeming control of her life. Robert looked around and then returned to his office and closed the door.

As Savannah drove home, she called Jonathan and told him what happened.

"Just come home. I will pick up Dominick and something to eat, baby."

"I think I may have lost my job now. I swore at him," Savannah said apologizing to Jonathan.

"Don't worry about that now. We will manage."

Jonathan picked up their son, Dominick, from preschool and picked up some chicken from the KFC down the street. When Savannah got home, Jonathan and Dominick were eating.

Dominick saw Savannah. "Hi, Mommy," he said with a mouth full of green beans. "Wont beans?" Some green beans fell out of his mouth. He grabbed it off the table with one hand and stuffed it back in and, with the other hand, he grabbed more green beans from his Spiderman bowl. He offered one of his favorite foods of all time to his mother with the juice dripping down his arms. Her concern subsided at the sight of her beloved son.

"Oh, you share your beans with me. Thank you, sweetie. You are a good sharer, but you eat them. Mommy is not hungry right now."

She tried her hardest not to cry in front of Dominick. He was such a sensitive child he would no doubt start crying as well not even knowing why.

Jonathan said, "I already booked a flight, honey. It leaves at 11p.m. tonight and your suitcase is on the bed. I didn't know what you wanted to wear so I just put in the toiletries and stuff. Do you want some chicken?"

"No, I can't eat right now."

No longer able to hide the tears, the dam broke and tears streamed down her cheeks.

Dominick asked, "Whaz wong, Mommy?"

"Nannie is sick, baby," she replied.

"Nannie is sick?" He parroted back to his mother.

"Yes, sweetie, I'm going to go see her."

"Can I come too?"

Jonathan replied, "No, you and I are going to stay here and take care of everything until Mommy gets back. Can you do that, big boy?"

As Savannah walked up the stairs, she heard Dominick sing, "I'm a big boy! I'm a big boy!"

Jonathan responded, "That's right and we have to make sure that everything is still okay for when Mommy gets back. We have to help her out, okay?

"Okay, Daddy. I can do dat. I'm a big boy!"

"Yes, you are," Jonathan said, as he hugged his son. "Stay here and I am going to talk to Mommy."

Jonathan turned on the TV and DVD player to his son's favorite Spiderman cartoon and left him at the kitchen table knowing that while it was playing, his son would not move.

He entered the room to find Savannah kneeling on the side of the bed quietly crying and praying. All in one gesture Jonathan put his hand on his wife's back and knelt with her on the side of the bed. He prayed silently. Savannah wiped her eyes and stood up.

"Jonathan, I don't know how I'm going to deal with this."

"Just pray and God will be with you. He will get us through this. I believe Mama will be fine. We just have to have faith."

Later that evening, Jonathan drove Savannah to the airport. She kissed her husband and he gave her a reassuring back rub.

"Everything is going to be okay," he told her, although not really sure himself. He knew his wife and that she needed those words right now. With that she opened the back door of the car to kiss her baby goodbye. It was a good thing that Dominick was asleep. She did not need for him to ask again if he could go. It was hard enough dealing with the unknown about her mom. She looked at the precious gift that was her son who looked just like his father as he slumped in his car seat. She stopped to take in the beauty of this little one. Although panic struck her heart, the tranquility of her son's sleep was refreshing. She kissed his little cheek and smiled at his Spiderman pajamas and slippers. He was holding his action figure that never left his sight.

Jonathan, sensing that she needed a nudge, said, "You need to get going, babe. It's going to be a long night."

Savannah acknowledged him and with one more kiss for her two men she was off into the terminal.

Chapter 4

The quickest flight to Atlanta left Savannah with a two-hour layover in Dallas. She tried her mother's cell and the hospital room phone a few times, but there was no answer. She did not want to take the chance of waking Dominick up at such a late hour, so she decided to call home once she got into Atlanta. After landing in Dallas, she sat in the nearly deserted terminal and waited to board the next plane. She prayed and cried out to God to not let her mother die. She quoted every healing scripture she could remember. She thought of their plans. Everyone was looking forward to her mother coming out for Christmas just a few months away. She thanked God for having such a wonderful mother and grandmother for her son.

As Savannah paced up and down the Dallas airport, she could barely contain her anxiety. "Lord, please don't take my mother, please!" she silently prayed. Although the layover was only for two hours, it seemed an eternity. She kept replaying all the conversations she and her mother had. What would she do without her mother? What would Dominick do without his Nannie? She turned toward the windows to avoid anyone seeing her. Rushing to the nearby restroom, she splashed her face with cold water to regain a measure of composure. Her arms ached for Jonathan, that man was truly her rock, a gift from God. He always knew how to make her feel safe. Although being with Dominick was more important, she needed her man right now. She pulled her phone from her purse to call him when she heard the boarding call for her flight. It would have to wait.

Settling into her window seat, she placed her ear plugs in her ears. Turning her face toward the window, she silently prayed. She didn't want to talk to anyone, but God. Savannah replayed all the misunderstandings she and her mother had over the years especially when she had "done her own thing". She realized and regretted every word she had said in anger. Her mother had loved her through it all. Somewhere in time, she became a good friend. Savannah could feel the warmth of her mother's embrace.

"God, give me another chance to hug my mother," she pleaded.

By the time Savannah collected her bag at Hartsfield-Jackson in Atlanta it was 10:00 am. She stood trying to clear her mind. "*How am I going to get to the hospital?*" she thought.

"Maybe I can call Estella." Oh Lord, I don't have her number in my phone she realized searching her contacts in her phone. The yellow bars let her know she was nearly out of power also. Reentering the terminal, she found the nearest rental car counter. When it was finally her turn at the counter, she searched for her wallet and she realized she had left her credit card at home!

"Jesus, Jesus!" she cried, collapsing into the nearest seat. With her head in her hands, Savannah's sobs shook her body.

"Are you okay?" someone asked, touching her shoulder.

Looking up Savannah looked into the dark brown eyes of an Italian looking man. She saw compassion in his face.

"My name is Marcus. Can I do anything to help?"

"I need to get to Emory Hospital right away. My mother's in the hospital there. I left so quickly I forgot my mother's friend's phone number and my credit card."

"I can take you. I live near there."

Savannah looked into the face of this stranger. She prayed, *"Lord, what should I do?"* God's peace rested on her, so she accepted his offer.

The new leather scent hitting her as she closed the door, Savannah settled into the passenger seat as Marcus placed her bag into the rear of the black SUV. As Marcus pulled into traffic going north on Highway 85, Savannah thanked him again.

"I don't know what I was going to do," she explained. "I'm so worried about my mother. I came totally unprepared with no credit card or even Estella, my mother's friend, phone number. All I could think to do was pray, and God sent you along."

"Yes, I would say He did," Marcus replied.

Savannah was usually very reserved in the presence of strangers, but she began to tell Marcus about her mother. She found talking to him very easy. This very gentle man allowed her to express herself anyway she wanted during their twenty-minute ride to the hospital.

"You were an answer to my prayer," she concluded.

"I'm glad I could be that," he replied. "Don't worry about your mother. She's in the Father's hands now."

Savannah noticed that he did not seem to take offense to her conversation about God and prayer. So often she got such negative responses, but she wouldn't change the way she talked for anyone. God was everything to her and she didn't care who knew it. She never pushed her faith on anyone, but she wouldn't be silent either. Her whole life, since she was a little girl, had been about her relationship with her heavenly Father. Just talking to this nice man seemed to bring her jumbled nerves under control. As he pulled up to the door of the hospital, a peace had settled over her. She knew whatever the situation, God would help her handle it.

Reaching into the rear of the SUV, Marcus lifted her suitcase out and carried it to the curb. She grabbed it and ran for the door. Remembering Marcus, she reached into her purse. Finding her wallet, she pulled out a twenty-dollar bill. When she turned back to thank this wonderful man and give him something for gas, he was gone! She looked all around, but she did not see him anywhere. She looked down the street, but there was no sign of his car. Standing there, she wondered what happened to him, but then pushed that thought out of her mind and entered the hospital. Marching straight to the information desk, she asked the receptionist for directions.

She followed the instructions and managed to drag her suitcase to the bank of elevators. At one set of elevator doors, she saw three men in close conversation. She caught only a few words she understood. What language were they speaking anyway?

"She's in the Father's hands now. We now have to protect her seed," one said to the other two.

Okay, maybe it was English because she clearly understood that. "*Wait . . . wasn't that what Marcus just said,*" she thought. It was strange to hear that phrase again so soon. That's a strange way to speak of someone's child as a seed.

"*Well, I guess that's the way they talk where they come from,*" Savannah thought. Looking closely at them, she wondered where they were from. They were from very different cultures. One was black, the other Middle Eastern and the last was white. They must be talking about someone dying. The broken English was throwing her off. She could not figure out everything they were saying.

With that thought, her mind went back to her mother and she prayed, "Father, please let me get there in time. Mom, you just can't die. Jesus, heal my mother." Shaking herself she thought, "*I won't allow the thought of not having her enter my mind. She's going to be alright. This has happened before, not for a long time though. But she will be alright!"* She let those thoughts slip from her mind as she internally screamed for the elevator to hurry.

"Do you know where the stairs are?" she asked.

Before anyone could answer the elevator arrived. As the elevator opened, the three men parted to allow her to enter first. Moving toward the back the wheels of her suitcase caught in the doorway. As one, they reached down and picked up the case and lifted it in for her. The black gentleman was nearest the elevator buttons.

"Five please," she said, but realized he had already hit the button on her way in.

One part of her brain tried to speculate on what three such men would be doing in the hospital at this time of day. They looked like they could be businessmen with their dark suits. Looking to her right, she took sideways glances at the white man and the Middle Easterner. She concluded they must be there to see someone they worked with. Who else would come to the hospital in a suit? They must work for the same company she decided. The bell rang indicating her floor. It drew her thoughts back. The three men lift her case off the elevator for her.

"Thank you," she said, rushing toward the nurse's desk.

Looking at the numbers she saw 548 and rushed in only to find the room empty. Turning to find the nurse, she nearly ran into a woman in scrubs coming in.

"Where is the woman in this room?" she asked, holding her breath.

"I don't know ma'am. You need to ask at the nurse's station.

Dropping everything, Savannah ran to the nurse's station.

"Where's my mother?" she cried.

"Who is your mother, ma'am?" the nurse asked.

"Bertha Henderson. Where have you taken her?"

"Just a moment. Was she in room 548?"

"Yes, yes!" Savannah said, panic creeping into her voice.

"Savannah?"

Turning, Savannah saw Estella. Estella! The tears started pouring down her cheeks as she recognized her mother's friend.

"What have they done with Mama, Estella?"

"We were in the room when they asked Raul and me to leave" she said pointing to a young man sitting in a chair with his head in his hands. Leading her to a couple empty chairs Estella held Savannah's hands as she explained. "They asked us to leave just after we arrived. We waited just outside the door. They worked on her for over an hour then the doctors shut everything off. That was just a little while ago. They said someone was coming to talk to us," Estella concluded her Spanish accent was very heavy as it was when she was upset. Tears covered her round face.

The young man Savannah noticed came and encircled Estella in his arms holding her close. When she was able to suppress the tears, she introduced Savannah to Raul, her grandson.

"Raul's a good boy. He brought me here as soon as he got off. He loved your mama too."

"What was the nurse's name that you spoke with?"

"Mitzi," Raul said. "I read her name tag."

"Well, I need to find her," Savannah replied, wiping her face free of tears.

There was no use crying. Mama was gone now. There were things that had to be done. All the strength her mother had poured into her came to the forefront. Savannah marched to the nurse's station and her tears finally stopped.

"May I speak to a nurse named Mitzi?" she asked.

"I'm not sure where she is. I can page her for you. May I have your name, ma'am?"

"Savannah Miller. I'm Bertha Henderson's daughter."

"Oh. You and your party may wait in the waiting room. It will be just a few minutes," she said pointing to the room adjacent to her station.

They all headed for the room the nurse indicated. Raul hit the light switch. A glaring white light revealed the vinyl-covered chairs were empty. While settling down to wait, the reality that her mother was really gone took hold of Savannah. All the thoughts she was keeping smothered came rushing to the surface. The tears started anew. Estella sat down beside her.

"Your mama loved you. She talked about you and her little grandson all the time," she said, patting her hand.

"I just talked to her yesterday morning before she went to lunch. She was fine. She was a little tired, but that was usual. What happened?"

"When she didn't show up or call me, I knew something was wrong. We never missed our lunch and shopping for our grandbabies. That's all she talked about for days . . . what she was going to get for Dominick. I just knew something was wrong. You know your mama. If she were going to be late, she would call. When she didn't call, I knew something must have happened."

At that moment, the door to the little room opened. A short blonde in light green scrubs approached Savannah.

"Mrs. Miller? Savannah Miller?" she asked.

"Yes, I'm Savannah Miller. Are you Mitzi?"

"Yes, I am," the blonde replied, taking a seat across from Savannah. She opened a file she brought with her.

"Mrs. Miller, I was the nurse attending your mother. Normally, the doctor would do this. But your mother made a special request of me so I'm doing it. I want to offer my sincere sympathy for your loss. Your mother arrived at the hospital yesterday with end stage renal disease, that's total kidney failure. There weren't any available kidneys for transplant at that time. We placed her name on the transplant list hoping that one would come available in time. We got her stable and resting comfortably after her dialysis treatment. When my shift ended last night, she was weak, but resting. Early this morning, before I came on duty, she went into cardiac arrest. The team worked for over an hour to revive her, but there was no response. We had hoped we had more time but..."

Savannah said nothing. She felt like a truck had run over her. She could hear Estella weeping. She just didn't have any tears left.

"What time did she die?" Savannah asked her voice just above a whisper.

Looking through the file in her lap, Mitzi announced, "7:43 a.m. was the official time of death."

Savannah realized she was at the Dallas airport at that time. There was no chance she could have gotten here before she died. A deep sigh escaped her. Bowing her head, the full weight of the loss of her mother settled on her. The dull ache reached every fiber of her being. She didn't even know how to pray.

"Oh God!" she whispered. She looked up realizing Mitzi was saying something, something she had missed.

"Excuse me, what did you say?"

"I said I think your mother knew she might not make it. She wrote this for you last night before the end of my shift. She gave it to me and asked that I give it to you," she said as she handed a white business envelope to her. "I am sorry, but I need you to sign some forms as the next of kin."

Savannah took the letter from Mitzi. It felt like it was the heaviest piece of paper she had ever held.

"Thank you. I can't read it right now." She wanted desperately to fall apart, but that was not an option right now. In cases like this, Jonathan would step in and take over, but Jonathan was not here. He was home with their son. She realized that her baby would be asking about his Nannie. The tears began to course down her face. " *Pull it together*," she told herself. "*You can do this*," she lied to herself. She did not know if she could. She never had to deal with anything. Her parents had taken care of her then Jonathan. She could not do this! This was not happening!

"The last thing she said to me was to make sure that I gave that letter to you and tell you that she loved you and everything would be alright," Mitzi continued. "She had such a look of peace on her face. I believe that she knew she wouldn't get to see you. She smiled and said again to me to make sure you got that letter. She was a remarkable woman. I know she must have been in pain, but she never complained. By the time I came in this morning, she was gone. It's just lucky she wrote that letter last night."

"I don't believe in luck," Savannah said firmly. "It was the will of God."
"That's right. Raul and I just made it in time to see her one more time." Estella said.
"I'm sorry but I will need your signature on these forms as next of kin so we can release her body and personal items," Mitzi said as she handed Savannah a stack of papers. As Savannah signed form after form, her brain could not seem to wrap itself around what was printed on the pages.

"Are you sure it was my mother, Bertha Henderson? Could there be a mistake? I need to see her," Savannah whispered.

Both Mitzi and Estella look sympathetically at Savannah. Neither answered her question. Mitzi took her hand and Estella pulled her to her feet.

Mitzi spoke. "I'm sorry; the body is in the morgue. You can contact the hospital tomorrow and tell them what funeral home you want to use.

"Tomorrow is time enough, honey," Estella comforted. You need to get out of here. Raul and I will take you to your mama's house. You'll think much clearer after you've gotten some rest and something to eat."

Savannah gathered her suitcase from the floor and Raul took it from her. The trio walked silently to Raul's late model Oldsmobile and Raul drove to Bertha's house.

Arriving at her mother's home, Savannah began to search for her keys and realized that Estella had already opened the door. Raul sat in the living room while Estella quickly prepared a meal. Savannah wasn't hungry but promised she would eat it later. Finally, after Savannah assured them she would be okay, they left with the promise to return in the morning. Estella hugged and kissed Savannah before she closed the door.

Savannah looked at the clock radio on the nightstand as she entered her mother's bedroom. It was just 4p.m. She felt like it was much later. A lot had happened in the last few hours. Savannah was so tired. Slipping out of her clothes, she slid into her mother's bed. Her mother's scent was everywhere just like she had just left the room. All the memories of how safe she felt as a child when her mother would tuck her in bed so tightly she could barely move. She remembered the feeling of the crisp clean sheets and wondered how her mother could keep them so fresh. All around her was reminders of her mother. As the memories and special moments came cascading back, she became her mother's little Puddin' again. The tears began to soak the pillow as sleep overtook her. A distant ringing drew her back to consciousness. Reaching for the phone on the nightstand she answered.

"Hello?"

"Baby, I've been so worried," Jonathan said, sighing deeply.

"I'm sorry. My phone died. Jonathan, she's dead. She's dead! I got here too late!" then relayed all that had happened.

"How are you doing?" he asked.

"I miss her so much."

"I know, but remember God is right there with you and we'll be there in a couple of days."

She said nothing.

"Remember your mother the way she was. She would expect you to be strong. Remember all the times she tried to prepare you for this. And, honey, you know where she is. She's not suffering anymore."

"You're right. I just needed to hear her voice," Savannah replied

"We're coming as fast as we can get there."

"Jonathan, I left my phone charger and my credit card there. That's why I had to get a ride."

"I packed your charger in the front pouch of your suitcase and where is your mother's car?"

"I don't know."

"I'll call a rental company and make arrangements for a car for you tomorrow. Did you eat?"

"No, but Estella cooked. I wasn't hungry. I'll eat whatever she made."

"Honey, just eat and leave everything else until the morning. Make sure you call the nurse and see if she knows where your mother's car is."

"Okay, I will. How is Dominick? Is he sleeping?" she asked looking at the clock that read 10:00 p.m.

"Yes, he's asleep. He was a bit fussy with you leaving the way you did, but I put him to bed a little early."

"What time is it there?"

"Seven o'clock."

"Give him a kiss when he wakes up. Tell him I love him. I love his daddy too," She said.

"I love you too, honey. Now get some rest. Don't forget to charge your phone so I can reach you. Okay? I will, Savanna said in a whisper. Bye, baby."

"Bye," she said, hanging up the phone.

She felt so much better after talking to Jonathan. Knowing he was there for her made her heart just a tad bit lighter. Finding her robe in her suitcase and the charger, she plugged in her phone and put on her robe and went into the kitchen. Finding broccoli cheese soup and a sandwich on the counter covered by a paper towel, she debated on warming everything up in the microwave.

An invisible hand touched the soup bowl and the sandwich. As Savannah went to place the bowl in the microwave, she found it was warm, like it had been just made. "*Strange*," she thought. What was even stranger still was that the turkey sandwich was fresh and the wheat bread was soft like it was just freshly baked. How did Estella know this combination was one of her favorite meals and how did she manage to keep it hot and fresh like that she pondered. Savannah dove into the meal. She enjoyed it. She did not realize just how hungry she really was. As she scarfed down the last bits of the wheat bread, she remembered she had not eaten anything for more than twenty-four hours.

Feeling the warmth creeping up from her insides, she sighed with contentment. As she put the dishes in the pristine sink, she thought how her mother kept the house spotless. She would often joke with her that after her weekly sweeping, mopping, stripping and waxing the floors, they were clean enough to eat off them. She rinsed and placed the dishes in the dishwasher, thinking of seeing the reaction on her mother's face, Savannah smiled. Her mother would have washed them and put them away so that's what she did.

Finishing in the kitchen, she moved around the house. Going to the living room, Savannah was drawn to the wall of nothing but pictures. There were pictures of Jonathan, Dominick and her. Most of them were of

Dominick at various ages. But she had one of Savannah's favorite wedding pictures as the centerpiece. There were more pictures of Savannah when she was young and some of her and her father the one summer when he took her deep-sea fishing. There was an old picture of her parents together. Her mother looked fat. She had never known her mother to be anything but fit with her 5'11 frame. Savannah wondered when the picture had been taken because she did not remember it at all. As she was trying to take the back off its picture frame, she started to cry again. The phone rang. She rushed to the phone thinking it was Jonathan, but it was a man's voice that she didn't know.

"May I speak to Savannah Henderson," he asked.

"I am she, but it is Miller now."

"This is Mr. Lieberman. I am your mother's attorney."

Savannah got very quiet and listened to the man tell her that Estella called and told him of her mother's passing and he was very sorry for her loss. She thanked him.

"I need to see you as soon as you can to discuss your mothers will."

"I did not know she had a will. She only gets my Dad's pension and a small disability check. She does not really have anything to leave. I even think she was renting this house. I will have to figure out what to do with all of her stuff. Do you know who owns the house?" she asked.

"We can discuss that when we meet. Can you come in tomorrow?"

"No, I don't think I can do that. I don't have a car and I don't know where my mother's car is."

"Don't worry about that. I will send my driver for you tomorrow morning at about ten. Is that okay?"

Savannah swallowed hard and said," Yes, I guess that's okay."

Reeling, Savannah called Jonathan and told him what Mr. Lieberman said

"He said driver?"

"Yeah that is what he said. That is some kind of service for an attorney."

"I will be coming up there before the end of the week and will bring Dominick, but that will wipe out the emergency fund and some of the savings," Jonathan said with a sigh. "Dominick is acting a little strange," he continued, "and I don't want to leave him with anyone."

"What's wrong with my baby? Is he sick?" Savannah anxiously asked.

"No, nothing like that, but he is just constantly talking about weird stuff like birds and yesterday after I told him about Bertha, he said she is okay. He said, 'the good birds took Nannie.'"

"Do you think he understands?"

"I don't know. At first, I did not pay much attention to him, but he is now scared of the 'bad birds' and whenever he looks outside, he starts to scream and cry about the 'bad bird' outside."

"Maybe they are teaching them about birds at school."

"Yeah, that has to be it. Anyway, I don't want to leave him here with Angela."

"Yeah, bring him to me," Savannah said nodding.

"Let me know what happens tomorrow."

"Okay, I love you."

"I love you, too, and we are going to get through this, baby. I will be there as soon as I can."

Savannah prayed for herself and for Dominick. She asked for God to protect him from harm. She immediately felt a sense of peace.

Chapter 5

In looking through her mother's desk in the study, Savannah found several awards and honors for her donations and service. She found clothes in the closet with the tags still on them from Nordstrom and Saks Fifth Avenue. One pair of slacks was $379! Savannah started to think her mother had huge credit card debt because there was no way she could afford the clothes in the closet. She went back into the study and saw a picture of her mother with some firemen and other people in suits with a fire truck behind them. She started to think about all the clothes, shoes and toys her mother bought Dominick and when she asked her mother how much it all cost, she would always say, "None of your business. I will buy what I want for my grandbaby and you have nothing to say about it!"

She discovered another document indicating her mother gave $12,000 to a dental clinic. She began to get confused and then angry! There had to be an explanation, but what could it be? *"The attorney will definitely have to tell me what this is all about,"* she thought.

Finding two boxes in the closet with journals in them, Savannah sat down and began reading the journals. The first one she picked up was from when Bertha was young. The next one was around the year of Savannah's birth. She read the day before her birth and two days after. She read in her mother's own handwriting how much her mother loved her right away and where the nickname Puddin' came from. Savannah noticed dates and times written in the margins of the pages throughout the journal. She flipped through the pages of other journals and saw the same thing. As she read, Savannah realized that her mother was writing visions she saw. The dates and times were when the visions were fulfilled. She found many, many entries over the course of her mother's life. Confused and weary, sleep finally overtook Savannah as she sat in a leather chair with the journals in her lap.

Angels entered the house. The beings touched the ground, one foot then the other, with such grace and gentleness. One by one each of them did the same thing. As they touched the ground their wings came to a point above their heads, gradually fanned out to their sides then finally disappeared behind them. Hundreds of angels descended all around the little house. They took their wings and fanned them back and forth creating a cool breeze. The breeze refreshed and made Savannah feel a little less emotional as she slept. The wings also made a sound like music and singing at the same time.

The next morning Savannah woke up in the chair. She stretched, feeling refreshed but a little stiff from the awkward sleeping angle. When she saw it was eight o'clock, she rushed to shower and get dressed for the meeting with Mr. Lieberman. She brushed her shoulder length hair and her teeth then sat in the living room and waited. She looked around the room. She went back to the picture of her mother looking fat that she had seen last night and tried to take off the back frame when she heard a car pull into the driveway. She looked out the window to see a black Lincoln Town Car. The young driver in uniform came to the door and rang the bell.

"Just give me a minute," she called out as she rushed to the bedroom to retrieve her purse and phone.

"I will be waiting outside," the young man responded. "Just take your time."

Thirty minutes later, Savannah was ushered into the very upscale office of Mr.

Lieberman. A small-framed fiftyish looking man comes from around his large mahogany desk to greet her.

"Mrs. Miller, it's nice to finally meet you. I'm sorry it has to be under these circumstances. Your mother spoke of you so much I feel I know you. Please take a seat."

"Thank you. I'm glad you know me, but I'm sorry my mother never spoke of you."

"That's understandable. But I need to inform you that your mother has taken care of everything. As you know, she wanted every detail covered. She was that kind of person. I'm sure you know this better than I."

"Actually, I'm very confused."

"I imagine you are. Let's start from the beginning. First, the funeral is already pre-planned and paid for. She is to be buried next to your father, Solomon. The funeral home will handle everything. The director will contact you about the arrangements your mother made and if you want to add anything to it."

"How did she pay for all this? I saw several pictures in the house that indicated she had given away thousands of dollars."

"Oh, I would say closer to a million."

"What! How is that possible?"

"Where did all this money come from?", she asked. Mr. Lieberman sat back in his leather chair and sighed. "Well, from what I understand your father left a million-dollar life insurance policy and your mother just put it to work buying a lot of real estate and investing in other businesses. She was a very savvy businesswoman. She owned three self-storage facilities and an apartment complex and the house she was living in. Your mother did not really talk about her business much. I handled a few transactions for her. Mostly, I took care of her philanthropic ventures. She came to see me once a month sometimes to just catch up and other times when she wanted to 'do something for someone', was how she phrased it, I would get the particulars and we would work out what she wanted to do. She never wanted recognition for the gifts so she would do it through me. Excuse me." He said with a finger in the air.

Mr. Lieberman picked up the phone. "Is Ms. Rodriguez here yet?" he asked the person on the other end. "Good. Send her in please."

Estella walked in and hugged Savannah.

"You knew about this?" Savannah asked her eyes wide.

Estella said, "Yes."

Mr. Lieberman explained, "Your mom asked me to set up certain accounts in your name as well as hers. This would ensure that you would have access to a lot of your mom's liquid assets without having to wait for the full probate process to be completed. I did this when I first drew up her will several years ago."

Mr. Lieberman read through the will out loud. Finally, he said, "Your mother holdings are worth a little over$3.5 million. I helped her get a $1 million life insurance policy with you as the beneficiary and a $500,000 policy for your son, Dominick Miller, to be held in trust until he reaches twenty-five years of age."

Savannah was breathless; she could not speak. None of this made any sense! "*Are we talking about my mother*," she thought. Everything was happening too fast. "What about her sister, my Aunt Rose?" she asked.

"Everything was left to you. Your mother asked Estella to be the executor over her estate. That's why I asked her to be present at the reading," Mr. Lieberman concluded.

Savannah looked at Estella and did not know how to feel. She started to cry which only made Estella cry too.

"I loved your mama. She was my very best friend. She knew she could trust me to see that everything she wanted done would be done!" Estella said as the tears fell down her cheeks.

Savannah asked, "Since she was your best friend, did she tell you where she got all this money from?"

"No, she didn't," Estella said.

To break up the emotion in the room, Mr. Lieberman said, "You need to decide what you want to do with the properties. If you keep them, I will draw up the necessary transfer papers. Here is the card for the management company. I am sure they will continue to handle everything if you wish. Just give Joe a call." He handed her a business card that read Sutton property management, Joe Webb and a number. "I will call ahead and apprise him of the situation."

"Did she have any other accounts or debts?" Savannah asked.

"I don't know about her other accounts or assets, but I know she banked with Freedom Bank."

"The bank can tell you if there were any other accounts" Mr. Lieberman said.

"You asked if there was any debt. I don't know of any and I doubt it, but I can pull her credit report for you."

"Ms. Miller, your mother was an unusual person. You don't meet people like her very often. She became a very dear friend." He leaned back in his chair and a smile came on his face as he remembered. "She would share pictures of Dominick when she came to see me once a month."

"Yeah, she would always want more pictures of him every time we talked." Savannah smiled at the memory. "Although she did not have Dominick with her, she said that she needed the pictures to take to the grandma brag parties when she went with her friends." At that Savannah smiled and another tear ran down her face.

"She gave a scholarship to my secretary's son through me because she did not want the secretary to know it was from her. When I was told of the death of your mother, I told my secretary what she had done. I am sure she will want to talk to you before you leave."

Mr. Lieberman stood up and headed to the door. Opening it, he escorted Savannah and Estella out. As Savannah was leaving the woman sitting at the desk came around to stand in front of her.

"Your mother always stopped to talk with me when she came in. And she remembered my name after the first visit. She would always ask about my family and how things were going. When I told her about my son, I was just telling her that he was getting ready to go to college. She was really happy for me! There are not a lot of people in the world who will share your joy with you. Your mother was a very special lady. She would remember and ask about all of my children. I'm so sorry she's gone, but her memory and the impact she left on everyone she touched, will never leave."

Mr. Lieberman spoke. "Ms. Miller, this is a lot to handle all at one time. Make another appointment with me for some time after the funeral and I will help you with whatever you need. The driver will take you wherever you want to go today. It is my pleasure to help you out during this time."

Overwhelmed and with her head still spinning, Savannah thanked him and left the office with Estella. The driver drove to Estella's house first. As she was leaving, Estella reminded her that she was as close as the phone if she needed anything. Savannah thanked her. Savannah looked silently out the car window as the driver took her to her mother's house. All the passing buildings and parks were a blur to Savannah. She still could not grasp all that Mr. Lieberman just said. She was so lost in thought that she didn't realize the car had stopped in her mother's driveway. She thanked the driver and walked slowly into the house.

As she plopped down on the sofa, she called Jonathan. She explained everything that had just happened. Jonathan was shocked. All he could say was wow.

"I don't know how I feel about the money. I'm still shaken up about mama. And I really don't know how I feel about the fact that she lied to me! No, I do know, I'm mad!"

"She really didn't lie to you. She just did not tell you," he responded.

"She helped all these other people, but never helped us! The whole time I was in school, I did not get a dime from her. I had to get scholarships and grants. When we bought the house, I had long conversations with her about it and she did not once offer to help us! She could have paid for the house!"

"Well, you know Bertha must have had her reasons, but you came out of school without any loans and we got the house without any problems. Baby, we are making it and doing fine. We have a lot more than a lot of people and you know your mother loves, I mean loved us, very much. You know she bought almost everything we needed for

Dominick over the past three years. So, she did help us out a lot. Maybe she thought you were strong enough to make it on your own and she was helping people who could not help themselves. Baby, you can't be mad at her right now. She did what she did. And you know that she wanted the best for you. Not to mention, she made sure that you were well taken care of," Jonathan concluded.

"Yes, I know this, but I am still confused and very angry!"

"Just go to the bank and see what you need to access the accounts. I overnighted your credit card to you so you can get a rental car and Dominick and I will fly in tomorrow."

"Thank you, baby," she told her husband. "I don't know if I could do this without you."

"You are welcome, sweetie. That's what I am here for. I will talk to you later. Love you."

"Love you too."

After eating her lunch, Savannah contacted the director of the funeral home, Donald Harris. He told her everything was prepaid and already taken care of.

"I want to get in contact with my aunt and allow her time to get here too," Savannah told Mr. Harris.

"We can hold the funeral next week. Will that give her time to get here?" he asked.

"I'm sure. She lives in Chicago which is not that far."

"I am so sorry for your loss, Mrs. Miller. Rest assured we will take care of all the details during your time of bereavement. I am your contact person and I will help you anyway I can."

"Okay, thank you, she replied."

After handling that Savannah found the driver still outside in the car waiting. She asked him to take her to the Freedom Bank near her mother's house. On the way, Savannah kept thinking about everything that happened.

"I just don't believe this. Mama, why did you do this to me? I just don't understand why you would lie to me," she said out loud.

"Ma'am?" the driver asked.

"I'm sorry, I was talking to myself," she said. "Yes ma'am," he said back.

At the bank Savannah asks for a branch manager.

"Hi, I'm Ms. Nelson," said a white woman with what could only be described as an afro. Savannah stared at the woman's hair. Her tight ringlets draped her round face and hung around her shoulders. The red color was just beautiful; she had a kind face Savannah thought. "I am the branch manager here. How can I help you?"

Savannah told Ms. Nelson that her mother just died and she needed to know how to close her accounts.

"Were you listed on the account?" Ms. Nelson asked.

"No, I don't think so."

"Well, who was your mother and we can see if you were listed as the POD beneficiary." Savannah raised her eyebrows. "The payable on death Beneficiary," Ms. Nelson explained. "Who was your mother?"

"Bertha Henderson," Savannah stated.

A strange thing happened. Ms. Nelson suddenly appeared terribly shaken and started to cry. She apologized and regained her composure. Savannah was puzzled by her behavior!

"Ms. Miller, your mother was one of our favorite customers. Was she sick?"

"She died from complications from Lupus."

"I am so very sorry for your loss," she said, still trying to regain her professionalism. "Let me see what we can do for you. Do you remember signing anything?"

"Yes, I think maybe some years ago."

"Well, hold on. Let me get the signature card. I am going to need your ID please."

Ms. Nelson came back very shortly.

"Yes, you are on all of her accounts and her safety deposit box. Here is the balance of all three accounts," she said handing her a note.

Savannah looked at the paper then at the manager. "Are you serious?????"

"Yes, that is correct. She had several large accounts with us. Ms. Miller. . . "

"Call me Savannah, please!"

"Okay, Savannah. This branch has a lot of wealthy customers and is one of the most difficult branches to work in. Most of them act like they are better than everyone else because of their money. They are very rude to us. They act as if they should be treated better because of their balances. And don't get me wrong — we do treat our large balance holders a little differently per bank policy. That is why your mother was so special. She was so nice to us! We just enjoyed seeing her come in. She would always want to know about how everyone was doing and about our families. We just loved her. She was truly a blessing to us. She prayed for me once when I was sick. All I said was that I didn't feel well and she stopped talking and grabbed my hands and prayed for me! I loved the fact that she never hid the fact that she was a believer. She was truly the epitome of a Christian. Ms. Miller, the tellers will be more than happy to help you with whatever you need."

She walked Savannah to the first teller and told the teller that she was the daughter of the lady that used to bring in the cakes, Mrs. Henderson.

"Yes," the teller nodded," I know who you mean."

"Well, she passed away," Ms. Nelson said.

With that said, all of the tellers looked at Savannah with sympathy in their eyes. Savannah talked to each of the three tellers and the two account managers before she left with a new bankcard and some cash. Ms. Nelson led Savannah across the room to another office with a young man sitting at a desk.

"Ms. Miller, this is your mother's personal banker, William Jackson."

"Just call me Bill," he said, shaking her hand. He explained that her mother had more than $1.5 million between five accounts and she had a safety deposit box in the vault.

"I'm a little stunned. Can you repeat that?" she asked. She had seen it written down, but hearing it, well...

Bill got his calculator and redid the figures. "Yes, a little over $1.5 million with all her accounts and we have the deposit box."

Savannah sat back in her chair and said nothing just trying to wrap her mind around what she was hearing.

Looking at her intently, Bill said, "I guess this is a shock for you."

"Just one of many since my mother passed yesterday."

"Oh, I didn't know it just happened. What can I do to help? Ms. Henderson was one of our favorite clients. Whenever she would come to see me, she would always ask about my family. She seemed like she really cared. We don't get much of that here. I handled all your mother's accounts she had with us, but she knew all the employees. Your mother was so kind. She would bake cakes and cookies for us and celebrate any birthdays or other important events. One of our tellers had a baby and she made a quilt for her. She is going to be greatly missed."

Savannah was overwhelmed. She nodded and began to cry. Getting up, Bill left the office and returned with a box of tissues.

"So, tell me, Mrs. Miller, how can I help you?

"Well, I need to get some money to handle some things."

"Well, your mother had three liquid accounts —two checking and one savings. The other accounts were her brokerage and IRA accounts. Please let us know when the funeral is. I want to attend; I'm sure others here will want to as well."

"It's next Saturday," she said, still crying.

"Which account did you want to withdraw money from and how much? You can use the new bank card that you have."

Savannah told him what she needed and he showed her how to use the new card.

Finishing up her errands, Savannah asked the driver to take her to the rental car nearest her mother's home. He was so nice driving her everywhere that she wanted to do something for him.

"Can I give you a tip?" she asked shyly, not wanting to offend.

"No, ma'am, thank you. Everything has been taken care of." He told her.

Those famous last words "everything is taken care of". How many times had she heard that today? She couldn't count. This was a mother she didn't know.

In the van she rented, Savannah looked up her Aunt Rose's number in her cell phone and called it. Her aunt seemed to be very upset to hear that her sister died.

"I want to come," Aunt Rose said, "but I don't really have the money to come."

"Oh, I can pay for your ticket. Mama would have wanted you to be here."

"Oh, you rollin' like that?"

"No. Mama left me some money and I am going to use that to bring you here."

"Really, how much did she leave you?"

"Well, I don't really know for sure how much."

The phone was silent for a while.

"Did you get enough to pay for the funeral?"

"Mama took care of all of that already." Not liking the way the conversation was going, Savannah changed the subject. "I was just calling to let you know when the funeral was. I know you and she had not talked in awhile. I haven't seen you since the family reunion, so I was just letting you know when to come down."

"Can you send me some money since your mama had quite a bit as you say?"

"Um. . . okay. I just met with the attorney and he did not know how much mama had. He only knew of the properties that she owned,"she explained.

"Properties? What kind of properties?"

"Three self-storage companies and an apartment complex."

"Wow, your mother was doing alright. So, go and see how much you can send me so that me and the kids can fly down there to be with you."

"Okay. It will be great to see you again."

"Yeah, yeah. Just call me back. Last minute tickets will be at least five thousand. You can Western Union the money to me. I am having trouble with my bank. They jacked me up and closed my account."

"Okay. I will see what I can do."

Feeling very uneasy after her conversation with her Aunt Rose, Savannah called Jonathan and told him about it.

"The one that was drunk and cursing everyone out?" Jonathan asked. "Honey, I don't think it was a good idea for you to have told your aunt about the money and properties."

"She is okay. She's family," Savannah responded although doubt nibbled at the back of her mind.

Back at the house Savannah started to feel the exhaustion overcome her. All she wanted to do was sleep. After a hot shower, she laid on top of the covers of her mother's bed and fell asleep. Savannah slept deeply while angels stood watch around the house.

The following afternoon, the call she was waiting for finally came — Jonathan and Dominick were at the airport. Savannah greeted Jonathan, with a hug. She clung to her man for a long time. She didn't realize just how much she needed him until that moment. Dominick was looking up at his parents and holding onto his mother's leg. She picked him up and covered him with kisses. When they finally got to her mother's house, they fed Dominick and put him down for a nap. Jonathan took over for Savannah and called around and found out that Bertha's car had been towed. He called to see what was needed to retrieve it and found out he needed the death certificate and three hundred seventy five dollars. Well, he could get it after the funeral. The main thing was to get as much off Savannah as possible.

The phone rang. It was Rose calling from the bus station asking to be picked up.

"Didn't you send her money for plane tickets?" Jonathan asked.

"Yes, but she said that she was at the bus station."

"I don't like the way this is starting, honey."

Savannah didn't like it either, but she was going to do what she knew her mother would want. She asked Dominick if he wanted to ride with her to pick up his cousins.

"Yesh! I bring piderman?"

"Sure can. Let's go." Savannah smiled at her son.

When she and Dominick arrived at the bus station, she saw Rose dressed nicely in a long sleeve leopard print sweater, skin-tight jeans with a black belt, and high heels. Her long weave was fresh and her pointed acrylic nails were painted bright red. The kids, well, they looked like the orphans you saw on the TV commercials. There was one girl, Tasha, aged ten, and three boys: Brian, aged seven, Edward, aged six, and Da'Shawn, aged three. They were all dressed in dirty summer clothes although it was the fall. Savannah and Dominick walked over to Rose and her kids, and Savannah started talking to Rose.

Da'Shawn saw the Spiderman and snatched it from Dominick's hand. Dominick began crying uncontrollably.

"What is wrong?" Savannah asked him.

All Savannah could understand between the cries and gasps for air where the words took, my, and 'piderman. Dominick pointed to Da'Shawn. Tasha took the toy from Da'Shawn and gave it to Savannah.

"Sorry," she said, "he don't have no toys."

Rose yelled at Da'Shawn as she snatched him. "You know better than that you little brat!"

People in the bus terminal turned to look. Embarrassed, Savannah rushed the group to the van. They all piled in.

"We booked you a couple of rooms in a hotel nearby," Savannah explained to her aunt.

"Well, I ain't got no money."

"But I sent you some and you didn't get airline tickets with it like you said."

"Well, I had some bills I needed to pay with that."

"We can talk about it later. Let's just get you guys settled. I know you must be tired," Savannah said with a deep sigh.

Rose grunted and pulled out her cell phone and made a call.

"Do you have clothes for the church?," Savannah asked the kids.

"Yeah we got clothes." Tasha said.

Da'Shawn opened one of the trash bags that contained the children's clothes and the only things Savannah saw were tank tops and more shorts.

"Do you have any church clothes?"

Rose stopped her phone conversation. "Hold on, girl," she said into the phone. "We don't have time for no church so no, they ain't got no church clothes," Rose snapped to Savannah.

"So, what are they going to wear tomorrow?"

"Ain't nothing wrong with what they got on."

"Would you mind if I got them some clothes before the funeral tomorrow?"

"Just give me the money and I will get them some clothes," Rose said with her hand opened.

Tasha looked at Savannah with pleading eyes. Savannah got the message and told Rose that she wanted to spend time with her cousins.

"Tell you what? I'll take them with me so you can get some rest in the room."

"You going to take all of these brats? Okay fine."

Savannah grimaced at her choice of words. She told Rose she had to make a quick call first. Rose grunted and went back to her phone conversation. Savannah got out of the van to call Jonathan and explain what was going on.

"Let's just pay for the hotel room and for some clothes," he sighed. "I don't want to let all those kids in your mama's house. Everything will end up broken, not to mention stuff just disappearing."

"I agree," Savannah responded. "Love you."

Savannah drove to a hotel near her mother's house and put them up in two adjoining rooms.

"I will be back in a couple of hours to get the kids, okay?"

"Whatever," said Rose as she dialed another phone number.

Three hours later, Savannah came back and the kids were all so excited to be going to the store. Thinking that the kids might not get much use out of dressy outfits, Savannah decided to just get the one outfit for the funeral, but also get each three fall outfits of their choosing.

Tasha told Savannah, "Thank you for taking us to get clothes."

Curious Savannah asked Tasha some questions and found out that Tasha's father wanted them to live with him and his wife although he was not Da'Shawn father, his father was in jail. After feeding the kids, they headed back to the hotel. Just before they get out of the van Tasha tells her brothers to give her their new clothes. Savannah watched as Tasha pulled the tags off each garment and handed them, along with the receipt, to her.

Puzzled, Savannah asked, "Why did you do that?"

"So that we can keep them," Tasha said flatly.

"What do you mean? I bought them for you, sweetie. They are yours to keep," Savannah insisted.

"My mom will take the clothes back to the store and get the money."

Shocked and horrified, Savannah couldn't wrap her mind around what this ten-year-old was telling her. After a few seconds of bewilderment, Savannah concluded that she knew what she was talking about.

"What does your dad say about all of this?"

"Most of it he knows but can't do anything about, the court says that we have to stay with Mama. Mama hates Daddy. That's why we don't go to church," she explained.

"Oh really, Why is that?"

"Cause Daddy is always talking to her about her getting saved and taking us to church with him."

"He sounds like a good father to me."

"He is! Mama doesn't know that I know, but he sends her money for us and she just uses it for drugs."

Savannah was shocked at the girl's candidness. "Your mom does drugs? You've seen it?"

"Yeah, sometimes she does not close her door and we watch her." She leaned close and whispered, "That is what happened to the money you sent. She paid Manny, the guy that lives with us now. He went out and got it. They spent the whole day in the room and I had to take care of everybody else. We didn't have no food."

"What!" Savannah seethed.

"It's not so bad. We eat at school." She whispered to Savannah, "I hate Manny. He is always trying to mess with me when my mom is not around."

"Why don't you tell your dad that you want to live with him?"

"I have and he says that he is trying to get all of us, but Mama. . . " her voice trailed off. "It's hard taking care of all of them. Mama doesn't do nothing but get drunk and do drugs with Manny."

"Oh my goodness," Savannah managed to say. Savannah decides to tell Jonathan all of what she learned from Tasha when she got back to the house.

Chapter 6

On the day of the funeral as the limo pulled up to the church. Savannah saw a large red fire engine parked across the street. Everywhere she looked there were cars parked up and down the street. There were six motorcycle cops directing traffic. Needless to say, the church parking lot was full. Walking into the church, she was stunned — the same three men she saw at the hospital were now standing behind her mother's casket. All of a sudden, she remembered their names — Jonas, Paul, and Fred — from their conversation. Why did she remember them and why were they here?

Savannah whispered to Jonathan, "Do you see those men behind mama's casket?"

Jonathan looked but saw no one. "No, I don't see anybody."

Savannah was confused but couldn't focus on them as more people were coming into the church and wanting to shake hands with her. The church was packed. There were so many people they had to set up folding chairs in the aisles. Pastor Richards came to Savannah and told her so many people wanted to speak, the service will have to be limited and if she wanted to say something, now would be a good time. Savannah shook her head and instinctively Jonathan stepped in to speak for Savannah. He went to the podium near the altar.

He began. "Although Bertha was my mother-in-law, she really treated me like her own son. My parents are both gone and when I married my wife, Savannah, Bertha was Mom. She was an incredible woman. I know you all want to express your feelings, but we did not anticipate such a large crowd. We need to stick to the list of speakers in the program you received. But for the rest of you, please write your condolences in the guest book, or in cards or letters. We will read them later. Thank you so much for taking the time to come." He concluded and moved back to his seat next to Savannah.

The fire chief, in dress uniform, came to the podium. "Mrs. Henderson was a friend of the fireman. She donated money to buy a fire truck when she heard that the old one was broken down and couldn't be fixed. The city was going to raise taxes to purchase a new truck, but Mrs. Henderson stepped in and bought it herself. You can view it outside when you leave. We named the truck after this great woman — we call it 'Big Bertha.'" Everyone laughed. "Seriously, the whole county continues to benefit because of her gift. Thank you, Bertha."

A police captain, also in dress uniform, stood and came forward. He began. "I got to know Mrs. Henderson through my son. When Mrs. Henderson worked as a teacher, she taught my son. He has a learning disability, ADHD. My wife and I had been told that our son would never succeed. When he entered Mrs. Henderson's class all that changed. She told us all that he needed was to discover how he learned best. She helped him succeed. He became a different child, excited about learning for the first time in his life. It changed our whole family. She went even further and set up a scholarship fund for police, fire and military service children that want to go to college in Carrollton County. She was an awesome woman. She will truly be missed."

The mayor of Carrollton was next. He recounted how Savannah's mom had established the Boys & Girls Club of Carrollton. "Initially, she did not want the club named after her, but we are going to change the name now to the Bertha Henderson Boys and Girls Club." That announcement drew a thunderous applause. There were so many people that wanted to say something about her. Looking around, Savannah recognized her mother's attorney, personal banker and the people from the bank. Savannah was overwhelmed as each person stopped to give his or her condolences.

Pastor Richards finally rose to the pulpit. "Thank you all for your wonderful comments about a very special woman of God. I think that there is nothing that I could add to all the wonderful comments made. Mrs. Henderson was a remarkable woman as you have heard from so many. She touched every one's life she came in contact with. She wrote her own eulogy with her life. Mrs. Miller, the church has received over 100 cards, telegrams and expressions of condolences. Because of time, we will send them with you to read. As so many others have said, your mother didn't leave us out. She is responsible for the beautiful new pews and lovely stained-glass windows. There is also a scholarship fund set up for students of this church who want to go to college. I could go on and on, but as I said her life is the best eulogy that anyone could write. I know you will weep, but not bitter tears. She is with the Father and knowing her, busy cleaning up heaven!" Everyone laughed.

The pastor continued, "Sister Bertha loved to hear Sister Janet sing so we asked her to sing a song from one of Sister Bertha's favorite artists, Cece Winans."

Janet got up and sang, *Don't Cry For Me*. By the end of the song, everyone was on their feet, including Savannah and Jonathan, praising, clapping, and crying. As Savannah returned to her seat, she noticed that her aunt had not moved. Savannah had not paid much attention to her aunt until then. The children sat quietly, but the scowl on Rose's face spoke volumes. *"She resented her own sister,"* Savannah thought. The hate in her face was unmistakable!

When the church service came to an end, everyone left to line up their cars to start at the gravesite. Four police on motorcycles guided the long procession, which had more people in it than the number of people in the church. The procession of cars was still coming in fifteen minutes after Jonathan and Savannah arrived. Savannah, while waiting for the brief service to start, spotted Marcus, her answer to prayer, her ride to the hospital. She was very glad to see him, but curious as to how he had found out about the funeral. Looking to the left, Savannah spotted her father's head stone. Now both her parents were gone. tears began to flow now. She had held it together, but now the reality kicked in. Jonathan put his arms around her. Marcus moved to her side and held her hand.

"I'm sorry you have lost your mother, but she is with the Father now," Marcus said. As he laid his hand on her back, a peace flooded her body. She glanced up to see a lot of people in the distance all in white suits all around the cemetery.

She asked Jonathan, as she pointed in the distance, "Who are all those people?" He looked and saw nothing. Then Dominick came to sit in his mom's lap and they both turned their attention to their son. The little boy took his hand and wiped the tears off his mother's face. "It's okay, Mommy. The good birds are here."

She kissed her son as she watched the casket being lowered into the ground.

Back at the church, a beautifully decorated room was packed with people. There was a variety of soul food dishes. Savannah looked at the buffet table at the head of the room. There were ladies dressed in red and black waiting to serve the people. The long table included baked chicken, black eyed peas, rice, ham, collard greens, macaroni and cheese and a plethora of pies and cakes. Savannah looked around and saw around fifty tables full of people. She wondered how this was all handled without her having to do anything. She felt grateful that this was just one more thing that was taken care of. One of the ladies in the red and black ushered them to one of the three tables with a reserved sign in the middle of it. Moments later they were served a heaping plate of food. Normally Savannah would have devoured the plate made for her, but she really didn't have an appetite.

People gathered around Savannah to talk to her about her mother. She learned that the red and black dressed ladies had organized the whole reception. They were the "Praying Mothers Guild" which Savannah found out that her mother was one of the founding members. They were a group of mostly elderly mothers in the church that had monthly prayer meetings for any in need of prayer. They also cooked for all the church's main events because they were the city's best cooks she was told. The older woman that was speaking to her about the guild told her that she and her mother were good friends. Savannah listened to the older woman who looked like somebody's grandmother. She was a short heavy-set milk chocolate skinned woman with stark white hair. She had a kind face and smelled like sweet potato pie. Savannah tried to catch the names of all the people talking to her and Jonathan, but her mind was in a haze. She mostly just smiled and said thanks. That seemed to appease people.

Savannah glanced around for Rose and saw her sitting in the corner of the room with a plate full of food. Her children, however, had never seen that kind of food before and were reluctant to try anything, but the potato salad. They stood around the food.

"I ain't going to eat none of that," Tasha commented.

"That looks weird," said Brian with a frown on his face.

"What is that?" said Edward, pointing to some ham.

When they were bored with looking at the food, they did what children do and started running around the room. Rose just sat in the corner texting and eating. Seeing the tiredness of the children, Estella suggested to Rose that the children might be more comfortable back to the hotel. Rose did not even acknowledge her so after a few moments, Estella repeated herself. She thought Rose didn't hear her. Finally, Rose looks at Estella and yells, "If you want to take them, then do that! I ain't done yet."

Everyone in the room stopped talking and looked at Rose and Estella. Jonathan rushed over to see what the commotion was all about. He agreed with Estella.

"We are going to leave now. We will drop you and the kids off at the hotel", he stated.

"Fine," Rose returned with a smirk.

Getting back to his wife's side, Jonathan informed her of the plan.

"I think we all could use a nap," Savannah sighed. After making their excuses to the crowd, they all left. Rose and the children piled into the van. After the altercation at the bus station, the two youngest were split up: Dominick sat on the second bench of the van and Da'Shawn's car seat was on the third row of the 15-passenger van.

On the way to the hotel Brian whined, "Mama, can we get something to eat?"

Rose's other kids chimed in. "Yeah. We're hungry."

Rose yelled, "You ain't eat nothing at that church?"

"No, that food looked funny," Brian complained. "They didn't have no chicken nuggets, fries or any hamburgers so I didn't eat none of it."

"Me neither," agreed the rest one by one.

"Well, you're just going to be hungry cuz I ain't got no money," Rose retorted while texting.

Savannah looked sympathetically at Jonathan. "Well, we can go to McDonald's if you want."

The children all screamed, "Yes, please!" They were all so excited like they were going to an amusement park.

Savannah whispered to Jonathan, "Can you drop me and Dominick off at Mama's first?"

"Sure, baby. Are you okay?" he asked.

"Yes. I am just tired," Savannah admitted.

They got to the house and Savannah got out. She opened the side door to get Dominick and Rose stopped her.

"I want to talk to you."

"Okay," Savannah replied. "Just let me get Dominick down for a nap."

"No, Mommy. I want to go to Donald's too," he pleaded.

Remembering the look on her aunt's face during the funeral, Savannah quickly decided it might not be a good idea for Dominick to be around. Once again Jonathan anticipated her thoughts and said, "I will take him with us."

Rose got out and walked with Savannah into the house.

The repast was drawing to a close and the people began leaving.

Marcus whispered to Estella, "Go and check on Savannah."

"Raul," Estella called, "I want to drop by Bertha's house to check on everyone before you take me home."

"Whatever you want Abuela," he responded. As they drove along, the pair was unaware of the angelic presence moving with them.

Estella heard Marcus whisper. "Pray for Savannah."

Estella said. "I hope everything is okay with Savannah. I don't feel right."

"Well, we will be there in a little while. You can see for yourself."

"Yeah, there is just something nagging at me. I don't know what it is."

"Maybe you should just pray for her grandma," Raul suggested.

"Yes, you are right. I will pray."

As soon as Rose entered the house, she immediately turned on Savannah. "I am gonna to need some money to get home."

"But I sent you $5000 for plane tickets and you came on the bus," Savannah said.

"And I told you I had to use that money for bills, so I am gonna to need some more money!"

"That was more than enough money to get round trip tickets for all of you guys plus some. I am not giving you any more money. I wondered why my mother never really talked about you and I guess now I know."

"Your mama wasn't all that! Yeah, she may have helped some people, but she was a hypocrite. She helped everyone, but her family."

Savannah had to stop and think about Rose's statement. *"Mama didn't help her so what she was saying was kinda true."* Nevertheless, her anger at her aunt was too much for her to bear.

"I just buried my mother and you are in her house talking about her? I am not going to stand here and listen to you talk bad about my mother!"

As she said this, there was a knock on the door. "Savannah, are you okay?" Estella said hearing the yelling from outside.

Savannah rushed to open the door and burst into tears at the sight of the older woman. She was so grateful for Estella. She clung to her for a long time and just collapsed in her arms.

"Oh, sweetie, it's going to be okay."

Unable to explain the situation she just sobbed. Rose and Raul just stood looking at them. After a while Estella said, "Come on, you go lay down and get some rest. It has been a long day. Don't worry about nothing. Just rest right now." She guided Savannah to her mom's bedroom and closed the door behind her. She walked into the living room.

Addressing Rose, she said, "I don't know what you were arguing about, but it's not going to go on. She buried her mother today. There is nothing so important that you get her upset all over again!"

Thinking about how Bertha was there for her at the passing of her husband, Estella's blood boiled at the thought of anyone hurting her friend. Although Bertha was now gone, her loyalty immediately passed onto her best friend's child. "Now you are going to leave with Raul and I and let Savannah get some rest," Estella said with an authority she did not know she had.

Unbeknownst to Estella, Marcus was standing directly behind her whispering the words she was now speaking. "I am not going to let you hurt that child! Whatever your problem with Bertha that is over! Bertha is gone and you are not going to start again with her!"

"Whatever!" Rose snapped as she walked out the door looking back. Estella thought she saw that Rose's eyes were yellow.

Savannah, now exhausted, laid in her mom's bed thinking. She thanked God for Estella. She had been there through all of this.

She prayed, "Thank you, Lord. She has proven to be a friend not only to mom, but to me now. I couldn't imagine how I would have done this without her help, Lord. God bless her for all she has done." One by one, winged beings dropped all around the little house. They flapped their wings sending a cool breeze that put Savannah into a deep sleep.

"I was with your mother and I am with you," a voice said.

Savannah jerked up and looked all around to see where the voice came from. Directly in front of her, she saw a huge set of legs and a pair of feet. They were part of a body that was seated. Then a hand dropped in front of her. Savannah left the bed. As she climbed onto the fingers, she knew that it was God. She could not see a face for the room was enshrouded with mist. She could only make out a robe and the hand she was in now. The hand lifted her to a place on the robe where she could get off and rest in the lap of God. She felt like a child again, as she walked around the lap of God. She had a thought. As soon as she finished the thought, the hand scooped her up and lifted her to breast level. She got off and slid down the robe screaming wee all the way down to the lap again.

She said, "Again!" like a two-year-old and the process repeated. She had never felt so much joy and contentment in all her life. "I love you," she said.

"I love you too, Savannah. I was with your mother and I am with you too," He repeated. "No matter what happens, you must not forget that I am always here. I want you to come to me with your problems first. I am the Lord your God. I alone can sustain you."

At that, Savannah was awakened by the sound of the door opening. Dominick walked in. Not wanting to leave this place, she kept her eyes closed. Dominick walked up to his mother and opened one of Savannah's eyes with his little fingers.

"Are you waked up yet?" he asked.

"Yes, sweetie, I am."

She opened her other eye and smiled. Jonathan rushed to get Dominick.

"Oh. I am sorry, sweetie. I told him to let you sleep."

"It's okay," Savannah said sitting up. "When did you guys get back?"

"About an hour ago, I had just dropped off the kids when Estella told me that she was bringing Rose back to the hotel. What did she want to talk to you about?"

"Not now, baby. I don't even want to get into it right now. I have to tell you about this dream I just had."

Chapter 7

"Wow, Savannah," Jonathan exclaimed, "that is amazing! Well, you know God is really with you. Whatever comes up we can handle it. I started heating up some food from the repast for dinner. It will be ready soon." He smiled knowing that his wife would appreciate his act of service.

"Oh, thank you, honey. That was so sweet of you. What about the kids? Did you get them enough for dinner too? I don't think Rose has any money left."

"I took care of them. I got them dinner for later and gave Tasha $20.00 just in case. That girl is something else," Jonathan said. "She is like the mother to the rest of them and Rose just lets her take care of them."

"Yeah, I know."

"Dinner is almost done so we can eat in a little while.

At the word, dinner, Dominick said, "We made 'paghetti, Mommy."

"You helped Daddy?"

"Yep, I'm a big boy, Mommy! I helped Daddy."

"Come here big boy and give Mommy a kiss."

After dinner Savannah said, "Dominick, we got to get you into a bath and into bed. I know you are sleepy, right?"

"Nope," he says, "I not sleepy, Mommy."

"Okay. Well, let's just get in the bath and get you all cleaned up."

After protesting once again that he was not tired, Savannah gave Dominick a bath and helped him put on his pajamas. The freshly-washed little boy laid down and, within minutes, he was fast asleep.

"Lord, thank you for the privilege of being this child's mother. Thank you for giving him to me. Help me to be as good of a mother to him as Mama was to me. Lord, protect him from all hurt, harm and danger. Amen," she prayed. Savannah kissed his cheek and whispered, "Mommy loves you."

She left the room. As she left, wings encompassed the little boy. Savannah joined Jonathan in the kitchen to help clean up.

"Baby, I got this. Go rest now," Jonathan suggested.

"I'm not tired."

"You sound like your son now."

Savannah laughed. "You know he is out like a light. It took just a few minutes and he was gone."

"Yeah, I know all of this is a lot for him. I am surprised he has not mentioned mom. Do you think he understands?"

"I don't know, but he seems not to be upset or anything. All we can do is pray for him. He is still young so he should be fine. It's me. I don't know if I am going to be fine," sighed Savannah.

"You will be, baby. God has us in his hands. He showed you in your dream."

"Yeah, I know. That was so amazing; it felt so real. All I could do was thank Him for the reassurance."

"I hate to bring it up now, but we have to talk about what to do with all of Mama's stuff."

"I know we do, but I don't think I am ready for that. Oh, that reminds me, do you know what Rose wanted to talk to me about?"

"No, what?"

"She wanted more money!"

"Are you serious?" exclaimed Jonathan.

"Yeah! She started in with me about how Mama wasn't this and that and how she never helped her. I was so mad. Mama hasn't even been in the ground twenty-four hours and she was talking about her. I ain't giving her nothing!"

"I hear you, honey, but what about the kids?"

"Well, I have not figured that part out yet. What do you think I should do?" she asked her husband.

"Well, definitely don't give Rose any more money! I don't know, let's just pray that God opens a door so we can help them. It's an impossible situation only God can fix it." Jonathan told her.

"So, what do you feel like doing now Miss I'm Not Sleepy?" asked Jonathan.

"I think I want to read some more of Mama's journals. She has boxes of them in the closet."

"Okay, go ahead. I will finish up here."

Savannah headed into her mother's study and plopped down in the oversized leather chair with one of the boxes beside the chair. She thumbed through a couple and picked one out. It was entitled The Vision Part 1.

'Spring 2002: God showed me a map of the United States. The map resembled the kind of maps you see in advertisements for airlines showing their routes throughout the world. The map was flat, but the state lines were visible. I saw that certain states on the perimeter of the US borders had bright lights in them. These lights were brighter than normal light and shot up in the air into heaven. At the base of these lights were less vivid beams that shot out and went to different areas of the world. Inside the lesser illuminations was a continuous stream of people. These people were landing in other areas of the world and from that end destination other lights were shooting up into heaven. The process continued endlessly it seemed.

I looked again at the original state map. In the states with the lights, I noticed that directly above there was a fierce battle going on. Angels and demons were engaged in intense combat. They seemed to be evenly matched. Then my attention went to the states with no lights in them. Above these states, there was no fighting at all. I look more closely at the interior of the state and could see that the demons were the authority in these places. It was hard to watch because I thought of the saints in these locations and worried about them. The Lord answered my unasked question when He showed me some angels with

the people of God and they were
protecting them from the demons. I kept
wondering how I can help the angels. I
looked more closely and I could
recognize some of the larger demons. I
saw violence, murder, homosexuality,
and lies. Like the angels, the demons
came in different sizes. However, the
smaller angels were fighting the larger
demons as well as the smaller ones. On
the demon's side, the smaller demons
could not and did not try to fight with the
larger angels. This battle took place in
seven different areas: Georgia, Texas,
California (two separate cities),
Washington, Ohio, and Virginia.'

The vision part 2

'I just passed exit 16 on Interstate 575
when I saw them. There were tens of
thousands of them. I had never seen
these angels before. They were riding
horses. These horsemen were wearing
long white robes. The horses were
white as well. But this was no ordinary
white. If I looked at it from one direction,
it looked gold and yet from another
direction translucent. On the body of the

horse I could barely make out a purple scalloped-edged robe just under the rider. In the hands of these enormous angels were swords. However, these swords were like none other I'd ever seen. I could tell they were swords, but they were not made out of metal. They were flaming swords of fire. The fire was not only red, and orange, but white all at the same time. These fierce looking angels were galloping full speed over the North Georgia Blue Ridge Mountains.

As I drove, I watched as this sea of angels invaded Atlanta. Once in the city center, they were using the swords to slaughter demons. They were slicing and dicing them up as they went, barely stopping. It wasn't even a battle. The demons were clearly outmatched. The angels did not stop. They kept galloping up the East Coast doing the same in the states with the lights in them as they went. This was no regular battle; the demons seemed not to even have a chance. They were being sliced up like they were weeds in the way of the mower. The sight of this was astonishing. For the first time that I had witnessed, God's side was on the offensive. This position has been unfamiliar to God's people for far too long I thought to myself. I watched as the horsemen made their way around the perimeter of the United States.'

The vision part 3

'Then God showed me the church I attended. I had seen earlier that angels surrounded the building. These angels were the larger ones, about 25 to 30 feet in size. I guess they were warring angels, but I have never really gotten clarification on the designation of the different angels or demons other than what it says in scripture. As I looked at the building, I noticed that these angels had been replaced with the horsemen. The horsemen lined up, side-by-side, facing outwards with their swords in hand.

All of the angels that I could see throughout the city were being replaced with these horsemen as well. At the same time, I could see more horsemen still coming over the hilltop. They rode into the cities with the lights slicing up demons as they went. At that point, God impressed upon me to look closer at the fighting. I saw that the angels were killing these demons unopposed. The demons had no way of protecting themselves. I saw the additional horsemen making their way around the United States. As the horsemen hit the cities with the lights, the slaughter began again and repeated in every lit city until the horsemen had surrounded the country and took their posts. With swords at the ready, these horsemen faced outward while other angels continued to fight in the cities with the lights. God made an impression on me that it was important to note that the invasion began in Atlanta.'

Changing of the guard

'I am in the hospital again. The doctors say that I have only 30% function of my kidneys. The sicker I get the more clear I can see this vision. Several doctors and nurses are in and out of my hospital room all day and night. I guess I should be concerned, but it does not seem to matter what happens to me because of all that I am seeing. I am not afraid to die which is what the nurses and one doctor seemed to think is going to happen without some kind of serious intervention. They questioned me as to why I had waited two weeks to come in if I had blood in my urine and my legs were swollen as much as they are. I really don't have an answer for them other than I thought it would get better. I did not tell them the real reason I finally came in. It was the daily annoying prompting of my best friend, Estella. By Wednesday of the second week, I was getting calls from her daily. I do not want to be here. I just got released a month ago with shingles and am not fully recovered.

Once in the emergency room, the nurse asked me how bad my pain on a scale was of 1 to 10. I told her 8 and she gave me some morphine. They moved me into a room, and I thought, oh great, I have to stay again. All I wanted to do was go home. I cannot understand why God did not just fix it like I asked Him to. This kind of stuff happens to other people, not me. I am not the sickly type. I am a fighter or so I kept telling myself. I asked God after puking on myself and the floor, why. Why is this happening to me? He brought a story back to my mind that someone had forwarded an email to me years earlier. The story was about a woman's mother that was sick with cancer and dying. The daughter asked her mother if she ever asked God why this was happening to her. The mother's response was one that stayed with me to this day. She took her daughter's hands in hers and said, "I did not ask God why me when the good times in my life came so I won't now". At that thought, I asked God to forgive me and then asked Him to help me fulfill His purpose during this time.

The hospital is full of demons. Some of them I know and some I have not encountered before. I recognized one, the one that comes from time to time. I still don't know the name of this one or why he shows up. I watched him follow me and jump from person to person. I asked God about this demon. I wanted to know why it followed me. His answer to me was that it was assigned to me. I prayed in my room and claimed that space as mine and the Holy Spirit was the only supernatural entity that could be there. I forbade one nurse from coming into my room. She had such a nasty spirit that her mere presence made me nauseous. I was determined that if I had to be there everything was going to be my way. The people here are supposed to take care of me, God's daughter.

The vision picked up just where it left off. I began to see the horsemen make their way around the perimeter of the United States stopping at the cities with the lights. In those cities, the horsemen would just massacre the demons that were in their way. I was truly inspired by the attacks. I wanted to tell everyone I knew, but I was stuck in the hospital. A few of my friends came by to see me and I told them. Estella came when Raul could get her here. In the back of my mind, I was still worried about what people were thinking about me after I told them what I was seeing. However, I was too excited to give much attention to the thought because God's army was on the march.

With the horsemen encompassing the entire country and standing side-by-side, they stopped coming over the mountain. To see this sight was so amazing to me that I think I got better just because I knew something big was going to happen. The horses alone were as big as the largest angels I had previously seen. Now with riders on them, I thought there was no way that the devil would want to attack this great army. In my ignorance, God reminded me of the last battle. He said that this was all foretold in His Word. I quieted my thoughts and just concentrated on what God was showing me. I saw that not only had the horsemen made their way around, but they also had replaced most of the other angels. The angels that had been replaced were what I called the big ones - warring angels. These were bigger than the guardian angels I saw with people. The guardian angels were about eight or nine feet tall. The warring angels were maybe triple that. The horses alone were about the size of a four or five-story building. I could not see the details of the angels' faces. All I could see of the riders was their eyes and they were like fire. The fire was a white-hot fire with a piercing intensity that I thought if I looked at them directly for too long, my own eyes might burn. I looked away hoping to save my own sight.'

As Savannah read, she was stunned that her mother had never shared any of this with her. *"Again, more secrets,"* she thought. She was so moved by the descriptions that she had to read more. She moved on to a new journal. The heading at the top of one page caught her eye — The Angel at the Church.

'God is still showing me things. I was at church one Sunday evening. There was a white man sitting on the second to the back row. I will never forget this man as long as I live. He had on hiking boots, shorts and a T-shirt. His face was unshaven, and he had dark eyes. It was not unusual to have a Caucasian person at the church. But there was something about this guy; I was drawn to him. I could not quite place it until he stood up.

A column of white light shot straight up
in the air. I was in the choir stand
looking at him as he stood. I knew he
was an angel in the human form. I was
not going to let him out of my sight. I
was going to be like Jacob when he
wrestled with the angel. As he
approached the exit door, I could see he
was only an inch or two from the header.
I wanted to run after him, but thought I
would look foolish. Instead I would just
wait for him to return. I watched him
turn the corner through glass in the
door. The restroom was the only thing
in that direction. I watched patiently for
him to return, but he never did. I
continued through the whole service
staring at the door and waiting. I
watched other men go towards the
bathroom and return, but this man never
came out. After service was over, I
asked some people if they saw him, no
one did. I was so disappointed that I
had not seized the opportunity when I
first realized it. I told my girlfriend what I
saw and she called me crazy. I have
decided not to talk so much about what I
see anymore.'

The prophet, church, and the demons

"That is a strange title," Savannah thought. "I have got to read this one."

'I went to this church because I was told that the visiting "prophet" could see angels. With a hope of finding someone else that could see them too, I went. I did not like going to this church at all. It was well-known for having openly gay men serving in leadership positions, and nobody says anything about their lifestyle. When I walked into the church, I could see thousands of demons embedded in the walls. It appeared to me like walls of black tar with a bunch of yellow eyes peeking out all over the place. I suppressed my apprehensions and went to see this man anyway. If he could see in the spirit as well, I had to meet him. I don't know anyone else that can see like me and I had to talk to him. I waited patiently for the "grand moment" — the appearance of the "prophet of God".

He walked in and sat down with great pomp and circumstance. It was a great theatrical entrance. It took three people to introduce him. As he began to speak, a woman walked in and made her way to an empty seat. I did not see her until he spoke to her while she was walking. He told her that four angels were walking with her as she walked in. I looked back and saw the lady and the angels with her as well so I knew he could see, but I did not understand why he was not seeing all of the demons. Then I thought if he could see one, then he has to be able to see the other. Why would he not tell the people that their church was infested with demons? I pondered this for the rest of the service. It was a revival so I will go back tomorrow to see if he says something...back from the service. I can't believe this man prophesied to some and spoke a word of wisdom to others. Not once did he warn these people. I did not understand why. I spotted a friend of my parents. I went to him and asked him how he was. I expressed my concerns to him. He told me he could see as well. I said, "Then why are you here? Why do you attend this church? How can you stand to be here Sunday after Sunday?" He told me that God had sent him to the church to be a light in this dark place. "Okay," I said, "I can understand that, but if this prophet can see the angels and tell about them, why is he not telling the people about all the demons?" He told me to ask him yourself. I told him that I did not think he would talk to me. He suggested that I write it down and he would make sure that the prophet got the note.

I wrote: With all due respect I have a question about why you don't tell the people of this church about all of the demons that reside here. I can see them and when you talked about the angels you saw I saw them as well. So, you have to be able to see the thousands of demons embedded in the wall of this church. Why are you not warning them? I am not trying to be disrespectful in any way. I just don't understand. I left my contact information and gave the note to my parent's friend. I waited and waited for a reply and none ever came.'

Jonathan poked his head in the door and said, "Hey, you okay in here? I called, but you did not answer."

Stunned that she had not even heard the door open Savannah blinked and said, "Oh, yes. I'm sorry. This stuff is fascinating, honey." Savannah recounted all that she had read.

"Wow!" was all Jonathan could muster. "And she never told you about all of this?"

"No. I don't remember her talking about any of this stuff. I remember she would say that angels were protecting us sometimes, but I did not pay that much attention. There is so much here, baby. I want to go through a little bit more before I go to bed."

"Do you want me to stay up with you?"

"No, you don't have to. I am going to be here a while."

Totally engulfed in the journals, Savannah couldn't keep her mind on the enormity of information that was dumped on her in the last few days. She rehearsed in her head all that had taken place over and over again. It did not make sense to her. *"First, daddy left a life insurance policy for mom and me, and mom not telling me about it. Then I have to wait until I'm twenty-five to get it. That makes no sense at all."* The more she thought about it the angrier she got. *"Well, I only have two months until that birthday,"* she thought. Savannah vacillated between sadness at her loss and anger at the betrayal.

She was more upset at her mother for keeping secrets. She didn't let her father off the hook though he died so long ago. Why did they both treat her like she could not survive without their protection? She never got into trouble growing up so why did they continue to treat her like she was five even beyond the grave.

Her relationship with her father was strained for years after she discovered that he had cheated on her mother with a woman at his job. She, at the age of nine, fully understood the conversation she had overheard her father have with the other woman. She remembered the arguments and when her father moved out and it was just her mother and her for what seemed like forever. After he returned home, Savannah was still estranged from him for several years. What made matters worse to Savannah was that the other woman was white.

Savannah decided then that she did not like white people. She went to a predominately white school where she would be called all kinds of racial slurs daily. Bertha did her best to instill self-confidence and love in her daughter about her skin color to no avail. The voices of her white peers were louder than her mother's voice. Bertha would tell her that her skin was the color of chocolate and everyone loved chocolate.

That was fine at home she would tell her mother but not at school. "Why can't I look like you?," she would say. Savannah felt that Bertha's latte coloring was far superior to her own.

Savannah grew up hating her skin color and the white people that told her she was not as good because of it. The fact that her father chose to cheat on her mother with a white woman was unforgivable to her. In her mind, it just echoed the fallacy that white women were better. She tried hard not to listen to the lies, but they still impacted her. From the time she was a little girl, she was told by everything surrounding her that lighter was better. For Savannah, fighting the feelings of insecurity was a daily battle.

Her father, Solomon, had tried to make amends with his daughter, but the relationship was never the same. Once back in the home, he had done all he could to salvage the remains of his family. He was thankful to be given a second chance with Bertha. Savannah had given the "I forgive you" speech her mother had coaxed her to give, but it wasn't until several years later that she really meant the words. When she truly understood the forgiving grace of God, she was able to give the same to her father.

Solomon had tried during his remaining days to make up for what he had put his family through. After losing it all, he had recommitted his life to the Lord. The restoration process had been difficult, but as the head of his family and the cause of the break, he had been determined to make it right. Getting a life insurance policy for his wife and daughter was his final attempt to do just that. He had thought that leaving them better off once he was gone was the only responsible thing to do.

As she sat in the leather chair, she thought about the fact that she had lost both her parents and they had been replaced with money. She did not know how exactly to feel. On one hand grief consumed her, all the while she was elated about having enough money to quit her job and spend time with her family. She allowed herself to imagine the possibilities that were in front of her. She knew Jonathan liked working on cars, but now he could own his own garage.

Savannah thought back to how they had met when her car broke down and she brought it into his garage. Once the owner told her that the repairs would be almost $2300, she just cried right there in the middle of the shop. The owner had no compassion for her, but Jonathan was smitten by this beautiful young woman. Once the owner left, he told her to have it towed home and he would fix it for half of what was quoted. He knew he could get fired, but he could not let her be taken advantage of. He was sick of the way his boss, Mr. Williams, would suggest unneeded repairs to boost the receipts. The way he ran the garage was totally against what Jonathan was taught and believed in.

Savannah continued thinking about her Jonathan and how he loved working on the cars, but coming to work was a chore he confided in those early days. He had to deal with his conscience. He tried to ease his spirit by telling the customer that the estimate was written up by the owner. He tried so hard to distance himself from even dealing with the customers. If he didn't talk to them, then he would not have to lie. He desperately wanted to leave that place, but he had to plan for that. He would discuss it with his uncle and get his advice.

Savannah's mind rehearsed the stories Jonathan told her about growing up. Jonathan's parents had died in a car crash when he was seventeen. Terrell Carter, Jonathan's uncle, took him in and helped him through his grief. His aunt, Grace, and his uncle reinforced the strong Christian values that his parents had begun. The love of cars and fixing them had come from his uncle. Even before the accident, Jonathan's uncle would spend time with him and his father. The trio would do all kinds of "manly" things. Jonathan's mother and aunt just laughed at them as they went off on male bonding adventures.

Uncle Terrell took Jonathan to car shows and taught him the basics of auto mechanics. Seeing the boy's natural inclination to the field, he encouraged Jonathan to get the formal training he would need to make a career out of it. Uncle Terrell constantly warned Jonathan not to take advantage of people. "You don't have to overcharge people for your services. If you do a good job, they will come back to you time and time again. Once someone finds out that you overcharged them for repairs, not only will they not come back, but they will tell others not to as well. You don't want to be that type of guy," Terrell had always advised the young Jonathan. "If you take care of people, God will take care of you. Especially women he continued whatever you do make sure you treat them right." "I know uncle," he would say, "my dad used to say the same thing."

Savannah remembered their first meeting. She was very upset and he just kept smiling and saying it would be ok. Savannah's anxiety melted looking at his smile and those dimples. He told her he would help her out of her predicament. He fixed her car and she asked him out as a thank you. Jonathan told her that he wanted to spend every day with her. Savannah smiled at the memory. His Aunt Grace, Uncle Terrell and Savannah took to each other right away. Within months, Jonathan and Savannah were in love and talking about their future together. Jonathan wanted more than anything to love and cherish Savannah. She reminded him so much of his mother and aunt he told her.

Savannah recalled calling Bertha and telling her all about the cute mechanic with the dimples. She told her how he had fixed the car and did not charge her at all.

"Ma, she said, "he would not even let me buy the parts!"

"Wow," Bertha had replied. "He sounds like a keeper to me." Bertha was not at all surprised at a call she got a few weeks later from Jonathan asking her if it was okay for him to marry Savannah. After hearing such good things from Savannah about the young man and having prayed on it, she gave her blessing. The two were married just seven short months later.

Now sitting in her mother's study, Savannah thought of Jonathan's devotion to her and their family. With the kind of money they had now, he would not have to work. But she knew her husband. Jonathan could not be happy just sitting around. She knew that he would be happy owning his own garage because they had talked about it several times as a dream that one day could happen. *"Yes,"* she thought, *"we will make that happen."* She imagined the building and an office and how happy he would be. He was a man's man, elated at the sight of a job well done. The grease under his nails and on his clothes did not seem to faze him. He was a blue-collar man and Savannah loved him for it.

Chapter 8

Excited to talk to Jonathan about her ideas, she got up from the chair, left the journals on the floor and rushed into her mom's bedroom only to find her husband and son both knocked out on top of the covers. Dominick must have woken up, she told herself. She looked at her family and thanked God for them. Even with the loss of her mother, she was still blessed, she decided. She glanced at the clock only to discover it was early morning. She decided to get into the king-size bed with her boys and get some sleep too.

Savannah woke up to their son's voice. She opened one eye and saw no one but Jonathan sleeping and decided to get a few more minutes of sleep. Being in a strange house she knew her son would not leave their sight. He was not an adventurous child; he needed to be around people he felt were safe. It took him a while to warm up to everyone. Once he decided that he liked you then you became his best friend. Savannah laid in the bed, eyes closed listening to her son. She realized that he was talking to someone. At that she opened her eyes fully.

"Hey, sweetie, what ya doin'?"

"Nothing," the boy answered.

"Who you talking to?"

"Just Paul, Mommy," he said.

"Who is that?"

"It's Paul, Mommy! I just told you," Dominick said frustrated.

"But I don't know him, baby. Is he one of your friends at school?"

"No, Mommy, he is one of Nannie's friends." He told her like it was the dumbest question he had ever heard.

The conversation woke up Jonathan.

"What are you guys talking about?" He asked.

"Your son says he is talking to one of Mama's friends named Paul."

Jonathan looked all around then at Savannah.

"You think he can see something?" he whispered to his wife.

"I don't know, but after all of that stuff I read last night, well I hope not. He is just a little boy. That stuff freaked me out," Savannah whispered back.

"Mommy, can I have something to eat now?" Dominick asked in a singsong tone.

"Sure, sweetheart." Savannah said as she climbed out of bed. "Let me see what Nannie has in here." As she said this the weight of Bertha's death came back to her. "Oh," she said, as she bowed her head. She paused," let's go out for breakfast."

"That is a great idea and we can stop by and see what time Rose and the kids are going to be heading back," Jonathan responded.

"Can you deal with her, baby? I just can't."

Jonathan interrupted her and said, "Don't worry, I will handle Rose."

They made quick work of the morning routine and were out the door to breakfast. Savannah told Jonathan about a restaurant that she and her mother used to frequent after church when she was younger. They ended up at the restaurant and the food was as good as she remembered. Jonathan tried shrimp and grits for the first time and loved the dish. Even Dominick cleaned his plate of pancakes, bacon and eggs.

Jonathan commented first. "Wow, this is strange to be able to go out to eat and not worry about the budget."

"Yeah, I know," Savannah responded. "This has been such a blessing, but I would give it all back if I could just have Mama back. I'm not really hungry after all."

"Okay, baby. We'll take it with us so you can eat it later."

Savannah sighed. "I feel so conflicted that my parents did not tell me about the money. I am so angry at both of them. How could they think that this would be a good thing?"

"Baby, you cannot be mad with your mom or your dad right now. That is not going to do anything but hurt you. Trust me; I wasted so much time being mad at my parents for leaving me. It took so long for me to get over what happened. I was mad at God for letting it happen, mad at the drunk driver and mad at my parents. You have to give God all that pain and anger and let him heal you.”

“If I just had one more day with Mama, I would do anything.”

“I know how you feel, sweetie. I felt the same way when my parents died. We have to concentrate on our family now.”

Dominick repeated, “Our family, our family!” and rocked in his chair. Jonathan busted out laughing and that made Savannah smile then laugh at her son. Dominick just looked at his parents laughing, and he started to laugh as well.

As they left the restaurant, Jonathan tried Rose’s cell phone, but got no reply.

“Let’s just go by,” Savannah said. “I know the kids at least got something to eat for breakfast because the hotel has free continental breakfast for guests.”

As the trio walked into the lobby of the hotel, they saw Tasha and the kids being escorted out of the restaurant which was in the front part of the building.

"Tasha," Savannah said rushing to her side, "what is going on?"

Tasha replied, "He say we can't eat in there."

Looking at the gentleman, Savannah asked, "Is there a problem with them eating breakfast?"

"Well, ma'am, the breakfast is for guests of the hotel only."

"They are guests of the hotel."

"Oh, I am sorry, the man said, "I did not know that. There was no adult with them when they came in. Sometimes we get kids off the street coming in to get a free meal." Looking at Tasha, he asked, "Why didn't you come down with your mom?"

"She ain't here," Tasha replied.

Savannah interjected, "I'm her cousin. We will stay while they eat."

Savannah rushed them to the nearest table and motioned for Jonathan to follow.

"What do you mean 'she is not here',"Savannah earnestly asked the little girl.

"I have not seen her since yesterday at the church."

"What?" Savannah said a little louder than she wanted. Jonathan, the kids have not seen Rose since yesterday!"

"Oh man, really! What have you guys been doing?"

"We just ate and watched TV," Tasha said very nonchalantly.

"Jonathan, the kids have not seen Rose. We can't just leave them here. Where is she?"

"I don't know, but I think Estella dropped her off yesterday when you had the kids."

After trying Rose's cell phone again with no response, Jonathan said, "Call Estella."

Estella confirmed that she dropped Rose off early afternoon yesterday. Savannah explained the situation to Estella as the children finished their breakfast.

"You can't leave them there," she said.

"I know. I think we will just check them out and get them back to the house and figure out something there."

"Okay. Do you need me to come by? I can see if Raul can get off work and pick me up."

"No, don't do that I think Jonathan and I can handle this."

"Okay, if you are sure."

"Yes, we will figure something out."

Savannah, Jonathan and Dominick helped the children get their clothes out of the hotel room and Savannah paid the hotel bill. The children piled into the van. By this time, all had been forgiven between Dominick and Da'Shawn. They sat on the front bench chatting in their three-year-old language not meant for others to understand. As Jonathan drove, Savannah tried several more times to reach Rose without success.

Savannah asked, "Do you think something happened to her?"

Jonathan whispered, "Yeah, she found a dope house."

"Shh, they might hear you."

"Oh, I'm sure they already know, Savannah."

"But still don't say that."

"Baby, she is what she is and until she gives her life over to God that is not going to change."

"Yeah, but maybe she got hurt or something. She could be out there somewhere in a hospital sick or dying."

"Okay, baby. When we get back to the house, you can call all the hospitals in Atlanta and see if she is in one of them."

Jonathan loved his wife, but her naiveté wore on him sometimes. She wanted to see the best in everyone even when their character screamed they did not deserve her consideration. That part of her personality made him love her even more all while making him scratch his head. As he drove, he thought about what to do. He needed to take charge of the situation or the kids would be stranded until they could find Rose. If they found her, would she be in a state to be able to care for them? She was proven unfit by leaving them in the first place. Jonathan decided to get in contact with the father of the older three. He did not have his contact information, but was sure Tasha knew it. *"As soon as we get back to the house, I will call him,"* he thought.

Once back at the house, Jonathan pulled Tasha aside while Savannah called the local hospitals.

Not wanting to alarm the girl, he asked gently, "Do you know your father's number?"

"Yes," she answered.

"Well, we will need to call him if we can't find your mother."

"Okay," she said.

After Savannah called every hospital in the Atlanta metro area with no luck, she relented.

"I don't understand how a mother could leave four children in a hotel in a strange city. I just don't get it," she said to Jonathan. "Don't worry about her right now. We gotta get these kids settled. I am going to call Tasha's father and see if he can come get them."

"Oh, do you think we need to go that far? Rose might come back."

"Baby, she left them in a hotel. Do you really want to leave them in her care again?"

"Well no, but. . . well, I don't know what to do."

"Let me talk to the man and see if he can come," Jonathan said.

"Okay. I guess you're right," Savannah acquiesced.

Tasha had the children in front of the TV sitting quietly.

"That girl is like their mother," Savannah said to Jonathan.

"But she shouldn't have to be," Jonathan said. "These kids need a parent not a little girl that was forced into the role." Jonathan's blood began to boil at the thought of it all. "Tasha," he called from the kitchen.

"Yes," Tasha said, appearing in the doorway.

"We are going to call your Dad now. Can you dial the number for me?"

As the phone rang, Jonathan thought about what he would say. "*Lord, please give me the words*," he prayed. Someone answered the phone. "Hello? May I speak to Mr. Brian Jackson?"

"This is he."

"Hi, my name is Jonathan Miller. My wife, Savannah, is your children's cousin."

"Okay." Mr. Jackson said.

"The children are here in Atlanta for their aunt's funeral. Rose, their mother, was with them, but now we cannot find Rose."

"What! Are you serious? Are they okay?"

"They are fine. Apparently, Tasha has been taking care of them since last night." Jonathan recapped the whole ordeal to the man.

"Oh my God! I will come and get them, but it will take me awhile to get some money together. Oh my God what am I going to do? That woman, my God! Lord, what do I do? Oh God, oh God, oh God! Baby," he yelled, "the kids are in Atlanta and no one knows where Rose is!"

"Hey, hey, they are okay! They are here with me and my wife in Bertha's home. We checked them out of the hotel. They are safe here with us. They are with family."

"Oh, okay," Mr. Jackson said with a huge release of air. "What did you say your name was again?"

"My name is Jonathan and my wife's name is Savannah. Rose is Savannah's aunt.

Her mother died and Rose brought the kids down for the funeral.”

“Oh, that is why she needed the money. Oh, I’m sorry. . . my first name is Brian and my wife’s name is Ann. Rose asked me for extra money to come down there for her sister’s funeral. I know how she is, so I bought the tickets myself. I keep thinking things will change with her so. . .” he let the words slip away with a long sigh. “I have tried to get my kids from her, but the court keeps saying no.” Jonathan heard the pain in his voice and felt for the man.

“Brian,” Jonathan said, “I don’t know if you are a Christian, but I am and you have to know that God has it all in control. Maybe now the court will give you custody of the kids.”

“Yeah, I am a man of faith,” Brian said. “I don’t just want my three. I want them all to come live with me. My wife and I both have been praying about it and we really feel like God has called us to open a group home for children. I know that sounds crazy because I don’t even have my own children with me, but that is what I know God is calling me to do.”

“No, Brian it does not sound crazy, but what we need to do now is get the kids to you.”

“I’m sorry I will need some time to come get them.”

"Can you get on a plane tonight if a ticket was waiting for you?"

"Um, well yeah" he said after taking a deep breath.

"We will arrange that along with your return flights."

"Well, wait do you know if Rose is okay?" Brian asked.

"We think she is okay, just out doing whatever," Jonathan said. "We just don't know where she is right now. We have to just wait and see. Meanwhile we got the kids from the hotel.

If you hold on, my wife can book the flight right now."

He handed Savannah the phone. Savannah took the phone and after a quick introduction she got on the Internet in Bertha's study. Within minutes she booked the tickets while talking to Brian on the phone. Brian expressed his thanks as Savannah emailed the boarding passes to him.

"My wife and I are so grateful. This may be the answer to our prayers of trying to get the kids to come live with us," he said. "I don't think anyone would stand in the way now. Wow. . . I don't know what to say but thank you."

Savannah could hear a woman in the background asking, "what is it"? and "Brian, tell me".

"I'm going to go pick up the kids," he told her.

Savannah heard the woman say, "What! Oh, thank you Jesus!"

"Brian, we can talk when you get here," Savannah said sensing his desire to get off the phone and talk to his wife.

"Oh, okay. Thank you again so much! You don't know what this means to us. I look forward to meeting you and your husband once I get there."

"Yeah, me too. We'll talk more when you get here," Savannah said.

When she hung up the phone, Savannah felt a warmth come over her body and a smile come on her face. She knew this was the right thing to do.

"Well done, Savannah." She heard a familiar voice in her spirit.

"Thank you, Lord for letting me do this. I give you all the praise for what you have done. Thank you, God for directing my steps. Thank you for your comfort, and God I thank you for the wisdom you will give me to do the right thing."

As she said her prayer, Marcus, Fred, Jonas and Paul appeared. They flapped their wings and a great peace filled the little house. The children watched TV in the living room and did not make a peep.

Chapter 9

Both Savannah and Jonathan continued to try and reach Rose with no luck.

Jonathan said, "Let's just stop trying to call her. What she is doing must be more important to her than taking care of her children."

"Well, maybe we should call the police. Something may have happened to her," Savannah said.

"You are right. We do need to call the cops." Jonathan picked up the phone book and dialed the local police department's number. After explaining to the officer on the phone the situation, he was informed that twenty-four hours had to pass in order to file a missing person report. With that news Jonathan thanked the officer and got off the phone.

"I don't know, baby. It just does not feel like anything is wrong to her. I feel like she is out there doing her thang."

"I know what you mean. I don't sense that she is hurt or anything either," Savannah said. "I just don't understand how anyone, let alone a mother, could abandon her children."

"Drugs are a powerful lure. I had a friend that was hooked on all kinds of stuff. Once he opened the door to that demonic force, it snowballed until he died."

"Really?" Savannah said.

"Yeah, he did not care about anybody or anything. It was like the drugs had taken over and he was not the same guy I knew just a few years earlier."

They were sitting at the kitchen table. Savannah asked, "Did you ever try drugs?"

"Well," Jonathan said slowly, "in high school after my parents died, I snuck out of my aunt and uncle's house and went to a party. They had some weed there and yes, I tried it and yes, I inhaled." That brought a smile to Savannah's face.

"It made me feel so weird. Now it made the pain of my parents' death go away for a while, but after I came down off the high, which I thought was not long enough for all the trouble, the pain just came back. My parents were still gone. When I tried to sneak back into the house my uncle was waiting for me. He asked me point blank where I had been and what had I been smoking. I could not understand how he knew, but I could not even lie to him. I just broke down and started crying. He just looked at me for a long time. He asked would my mom and dad be pleased with my behavior right now. That was the first and only time my uncle looked at me with disappointment in his eyes. I felt so bad. I mean I felt like dirt. I admired him, still do, and although he was not my father, he and my aunt were all I had left in the world. I begged him not to tell my aunt and told him I would never do it again. He kept his word and I never touched the stuff again."

"Wow, you never told me that story before," Savannah said.

"No, that is part of a past that I don't ever want to relive. Have you ever done anything like that, that I don't know about?"

"Well, I never did any drugs and alcohol. I was too into clothes and boys."

"Oh, you were a goody two shoes!"

"I guess you could say that. I just was not into that crowd. Well, I take that back. The year my Dad was gone, I drank a little, but not much. My girlfriends were going to this party and I wanted to go too. So, I lied to my mama about where I was going to be and went to the party. They had beer there and I drank some and some punch that they put God knows what in. I didn't really like the taste of it so that was the beginning and end of my drinking."

"Well, I'm glad I married a good girl," Jonathan smiled.

"You wouldn't have married me if I had a really bad past?"

"Well, no," Jonathan said. "I asked God for what I wanted and He gave me just what I wanted and needed in you."

"Wow, baby, that was a nice cleanup," Savannah said with a grin.

"You know how I do," Jonathan said smiling back. Savannah looked at her husband and thought I love that smile and those dimples, so she kissed him.

"Let's do something with the kids," Savannah suggested as she looked into the living room.

"I don't know what is open right now, in the middle of the day for children. Kids are in school." Jonathan remarked.

"Well, maybe the movies," Savannah returned. Dominick heard movies and just kept repeating movies, movies.

"Oh, can we go?" The children said in unison. They all jumped up and ran into the kitchen.

Jonathan laughed, "That's your boy in there!" Savannah looked at Jonathan. "You know you can't talk that loud with him around. Well, I guess we are going to the movies."

After the movie and lunch they all arrive back at the house exhausted. All the kids sprawled out on the living room floor to watch TV when the phone rang.

"Estella is calling to check up on you, Savannah," Jonathan said as he looked at the phone. Savannah picks up the receiver of her mother's old school landline phone.
"Hello? How are you doing niña?" asked Estella.

"I'm doing fine except we can't find Rose anywhere," Savannah reported.

"What! Are you serious? Esa mujer tonta. Dejar a los niños solos es simplemente impensable. Señor, por favor ayuda."

"What?" Savannah said.

"Oh, sweetie, I'm sorry. It's nothing. We will come over and help with the kids. I just do not understand how anyone can just run off and leave their kids. I just do not.... *¿Por qué ella haría esto ahora? Bertha acababa de morir. Señor, me da fuerza, ayudarme no para matarla cuando encontrarla.*"

"Estella, Estella it's okay. We called the kids' father and he is coming to pick them up tomorrow."

"Oh, thank you, God. We will come in a few minutes." Suddenly the phone went dead.

"Estella, are you there?" After a few seconds Savannah just hung up the phone.

Jonathan looked at Savannah and waited for her to speak. Savannah just shook her head and said Estella and Raul were on the way over.

"What else did she say?" he asked.

"I have no idea. She went off in Spanish. She was probably cussing Rose out. Baby, I am glad I have you and her because I don't know if I could do this by myself."

"See, God did not leave you alone."

At his words Savannah broke down, her eyes filled with tears and she collapsed in the middle of the floor. Jonathan went to her and just held her for a moment.

Time stood still as the four angels came to encircle Savannah and Jonathan. As each one touched their heads, virtue and strength came into both of them. God spoke to them simultaneously. From the depths of their souls they both heard, "I will never leave you nor forsake you. All things on this earth will pass away. Only My kingdom will endure forever. This trial is for your good. It will strengthen you to do what I have called you to do. Savannah, I have known you since before you were born. I knew your beginning and I know your end. You are precious to me and I have you in my hands. You have much work to do. I have equipped you for the task and I have given you help to accomplish it. Wait on My leading and My voice and I will tell you what to do. Jonathan, help your wife, the woman I have given to you. She will help you to accomplish the tasks I have for your family. Do not give in to the tricks of the enemy. He will try and bring depression, loneliness, and confusion to you. There is no time to delay with these things. Let your heart grieve your loss, but don't stay there. It is a demonic spirit that wants you to wallow in grief and sadness and not move past it. You have the power within you to fight it. You must praise Me in the midst of your pain."

Marcus, Paul, Jonas, and Fred stepped back and allowed the Holy Spirit to touch Savannah. As He did, the glory of the Lord filled the whole house. Golden rain flowed from heaven and drenched the house. The four along with the Spirit of God moved to each occupant and touched their heads. The golden rain stopped, and a mist took its place. God dealt with each person, comforting, encouraging, and charging as needed. The Spirit lifted and the four angels lifted Savannah to her feet and placed her in a chair at the kitchen table again.

Time resumed and all were oblivious to the presence of the Lord's ministering angels. All just felt the most intense happiness and joy. Dominick was the first to speak.

"Mommy, I happy. You happy too?" he asked as he climbed into her lap.

"Yes, baby, Mommy is happy too."

He took his hands and framed her face and said, "It was the good birds, Mommy. You were sad and the good birds came and made you happy. I asked them to make you happy, Mommy, and they did."

"Thank you, sweetheart," she said then looked at Jonathan. He shrugged his shoulders. Savannah kissed her son and held him for a while.

"I love you so much," she told him.

"I know dat. I lub you too."

The boy sat in his mother's lap and just loved her back. The gifts God had placed on the young child were at work already, but no one knew.

A few moments later Raul and Estella rang the doorbell. They stayed and visited for an hour.

Suddenly, Da'Shawn moaned, "I'm hungry. You got any food?"

Tasha looked at him and said, "Shut up. You just ate. You don't be askin' fo' no food like that."

"It's okay, Tasha," Savannah said. "If you are hungry, you can say so."

"But my momma said she would beat us if she found out we were beggin'. It would be me that got it, not them and I ain't takin' no ass whoopin' for none of these little brats."

All the adults looked at Tasha with great astonishment at the magnitude of what she said.

Savannah spoke first. "Baby, it's not nice to swear or call your brothers brats. That is not good at all. I don't want to hear you use that kind language anymore, okay?"

"Yes, but I'm the one who is going to be in trouble, not them."

"It's okay. Nobody is going to tell your mother, are we kids?"

"No," everyone including Dominick said in unison.

"Is everybody else hungry? It was nearly one," Estella said. She felt a tiny hand patting her leg.

"Miss Ella can we get some beans?" Dominick asked, trying to pronounce Estella's name.

"You want beans, baby?"

"He wants green beans from KFC," Savannah explained.

"Sure, you can have some beans," Estella said cupping his little face in her hand then kissing his dimpled cheeks as he smiled. "Would you all like KFC too?" she asked all the kids

"Yes, please!" Tasha responded for them. "We have never had KFC before. Can we get some chicken too?"

Their eyes sparkled with excitement. The adults laughed.

"Yes, you can get some chicken," Jonathan chuckled.

Estella's heart went out to these children. She thought, "I am sure Bertha didn't know how bad her sister treated these babies or she would have done something!"

Jonathan announced, "I saw a KFC up the street."

Estella stated, "Oh, you mean the Big Chicken?"

"Big Chicken?" Jonathan and Savannah said in unison. "Yes, the KFC has a big chicken on top of it. It's a landmark in Marietta." Estella explained. "Okay, the big chicken it is." Jonathan stated.

"Big chicken, big chicken, we goin' to the big chicken!" Brian sang.

Raul helped the kids into the van then looked at Estella and said, "I need to get to work, Abuela."

"Okay, go to work, nieto. I will get a ride home. She said out loud to herself, "Such a good boy."

"Do you feel like coming?" Jonathan asked Savannah who was standing by the van.

"Yeah, I guess."

Just as Raul was pulling out of the driveway, another car pulled in and blocked the van. Rose hopped out of the passenger side and yelled, "Where is my kids?"

Jonathan finished fastening Dominick and Da'Shawn into their car seats and looked up.

Rose yelled, "Savannah, I know you did this! You are trying to take my kids away from me!"

"Mama, they just took us to get something to eat," Tasha said.

"Don't give me that shit, Tasha. I know they had free breakfast at the hotel."

"But they would not let us eat it because you were not there. Then Jonathan and Savannah came so they let us eat."

"So why are we checked out of the hotel then?"

Before Tasha could answer Jonathan said, "You left them alone and we have been trying to get you on the phone, but you would not answer it."

Ignoring Jonathan, Rose yelled, "Tasha, get in the damn car!"

Jonathan stepped in front of her and directed, "No. Get in the van, Tasha."

Tasha stood there not knowing what to do.

Savannah stepped behind Tasha and murmured, "Get in the van. It's okay."

"Tasha, if you don't get in this goddamn car, I'm going to beat your ass!"

"Oh, God, helps us, Lord!" Savannah silently prayed.

"Oh Dios, *hacer esta mala mujer sólo tienes que ir y dejar estos bebés solos. Ayúdanos Señor, haz que esta mujer desaparece. Jesús,*" Estella also silently prayed. "Oh, that woman!" she said as she grabbed Tasha 's hand and helped her into the van.

"No! I got to go with her," Tasha protested, "or we all are gonna' to get it."

"Nothing is going to happen to you. We made sure of it," Savannah reassured Tasha. "Your Dad is coming so you won't even be living with her anymore." As she said these words, a determination to protect these children came over her.

Marcus moved from his location at the front door to stand directly in front of Jonathan. Adonis, now fully indwelt in Rose, knew that as long as the women were praying he could not win this battle. Rose railed insults at Savannah and Jonathan trying hard to get the women to stop praying. Jonathan put his hands on both Estella and Savannah's arms and stepped in front of them just as Savannah was about to speak. In a last-ditch effort, Rose became agitated and said "You think your mom was so great why didn't she help her own family. She was a hypocrite! Always acting like she was better than everyone else. I hated her and I hate you!" He succeeded in stopping the praying. Both now engaged Rose and a shouting match ensued in the middle of the driveway. Paul, Fred and Jonas gathered around the women to calm them and continued to speak words of peace and bring scripture to their remembrance. Because of all the commotion, the neighbors called the police. The driver of the car Rose was in heard the sirens and told her that he had to go. Ignoring him, Rose continued to yell insults at Savannah. Since drugs were in the car, the driver shouted to Rose that he was leaving with or without her. She decided to leave with him.

Jonathan turned to his wife, "Are you okay?"

"Yes, but I don't understand why she is so mad with me and Mama."

"Baby, don't worry about it. You are not going to be able to reason with her. She is probably high right now. Nothing you say is going to do any good. This is not one of those cases where you can sit down and talk it out. I know that is what you want to do, but you are not going to resolve this. Just let me handle her from now on. Don't even engage her in conversation."

"Okay, I won't, but I just don't get why she is so mad at me. I hardly know her."

Jonathan sighed. "Savannah, think about it. Your mom left you money and she wants it. People like that always want the easy way. They want others to give them something instead of working for it. They think that if you have something then that means that you took it from someone else or that you should give it to them. It's the Robin Hood mentality that has taken root in too many people's minds. If you are wealthy, then you must have done something bad to get it. She just wants someone to blame for what she is going through, but she is the only one to blame."

"Shh, baby, the kids might hear you. It's a good thing their father is coming to get them. There is no telling what that woman would do to the kids in this state."

Jonathan, Savannah and Estella talked with the police for a little while and assured them and the neighbors who had emerged from their homes that everything was under control. They drove to KFC. Everyone, including Dominick, was silent. The kids ate lunch and Jonathan purchased some extra food for dinner knowing that nobody felt like cooking after the run in with Rose. Besides, the only food in the house was the remainder of the food from the repast that the kids would not eat. Not wanting to waste it Savannah asked Estella to take it back to the seniors where she lived.

"I will have to sneak it in, but most of the ladies have little refrigerators in their rooms. I do, but it won't all fit in mine. I will work it out though. It won't go to waste."

"Okay, good," Savannah said. "I just don't want it to sit and go bad. Jonathan, and Dominick won't eat this much food before it goes bad and I haven't really felt like eating much of anything."

Savannah looked at Jonathan and asked, "Is that alright, baby?"

"Yes, that is fine sweetheart, but I do want you to try and eat something. You really didn't eat that much of your breakfast. I know you are upset, but I don't want you to get sick as well."

"Okay," Savannah said, "I will try."

"Savannah, listen to your husband. He is telling you the truth," Estella encouraged.

"Yes, yes. I will eat." She downed a piece of chicken and half of a biscuit to the satisfied looks of both Jonathan and Estella.

"Thank you, babe. I know you did not want to do that, but you needed it. Now let's get back. The kids are getting restless."

Jonathan drove back to the house. Savannah went to lie down while Jonathan, Estella and Tasha got the kids settled down. Jonathan put Da'Shawn and Dominick down for a nap while the other kids watched TV in the living room. After giving instructions to let Savannah sleep, Jonathan drove Estella, and the repast leftovers, home at the assisted-living facility. Jonathan stayed and met several women who knew Bertha and wanted to convey their condolences to him and Savannah. He stayed for about an hour then stood to leave giving his apologies. The women protested and the only way he could get away was to tell them he had to see about his wife. The women reluctantly let him leave expressing their condolences again.

Chapter 10

Marcus and the other angels encircled the house once again and began flapping their wings, which produced music and a soft breeze. The older children were content and watched TV more peaceful than ever before. The wind allowed the sleepers the most restful sleep they had had in a long time. Even the two young ones did not fuss or try and stay awake; they just drifted off into tranquility. While asleep, Savannah dreamt about her mother.

"Mama, why did you leave me?" she cried.

Bertha was standing before her and answered, "Puddin', you are not a baby anymore. You are strong enough to make it on your own."

"I'm not strong," she protested.

"I remained because of you. I did what I needed to do and now it is your turn. Take what I gave you and bless others. Help fund the Kingdom of God and prosper. God has much for you to do. Always remember who you are, Savannah. God has given you so many gifts and you are to use them for His glory."

With those words, Bertha disappeared, and Savannah was left in a field of tall grass. She sat down and began to cry.

"I don't want this, God. Just bring my mother back, please," she begged. Bertha never returned and Savannah sat oblivious to the hundreds of angelic beings around her.

"God, why have you done this to me? Why did you leave me all alone?"

Her words just hang in the air. Her heart just poured out all of the anger, bitterness, and sadness that was bottled up inside. In her sleep, Savannah grieved for her mother and all she had lost.

Savannah rolled over and snuggled deeper into the covers.

By dinnertime, Jonathan and Tasha had the house running like a well-oiled machine. The children ate and took turns taking a bath and getting ready for bed. Savannah woke up and walked slowly into the kitchen.

"What time is it? How long was I asleep?" she asked groggily.

"It's almost seven, baby. I told everyone to be quiet and let you sleep. Are you hungry yet? We still have some chicken."

"No, I'm not hungry, where is Dominick?"

"He is in the bath with Da'Shawn. Tasha is getting them ready for bed."

"Oh," she said as she plopped down on the kitchen chair.

"I had the strangest dream, but I don't remember all of it. I just remember talking to Mama and then she was gone."

"What did she say?" Jonathan asked.

"I don't really remember everything, just that she was telling me to remember who I was. What do you think she meant by that?"

"I don't know, babe, but obviously she is still looking out for you even from heaven."

"Yeah, I guess you are right."

Dominick walked into the kitchen in his underwear and said, "Mommy, are you all waked up now?"

"Yes, baby, I'm awake, but you need your PJs and slippers."

"They in the bafroom, Mommy." The little boy said.

"Okay, then go get them and bring them to me so I can help you put them on."

"No, Mommy, I can do it myself. I a big boy."

"Okay, big boy, get to getting!"

Dominick ran down the hall as fast as his little legs could go. A few moments later, he emerged fully dressed along with Da'Shawn dressed in a t-shirt, underwear and socks. Tasha followed all wet.

"Looks like you two had fun getting Tasha all wet." Jonathan stated with a grin.

"Yep!" The two just looked at each other and started giggling.

"Dominick, you did that on purpose," Savannah scolded.

"I sorry," he said.

"Don't tell me. Tell your cousin."

With his head bowed down, he walked to Tasha with tears in his eyes. "I sorry."

"It's okay," she said. "I'm used to it, but you two got my hair wet. Now it's going to be nappy."

Jonathan looked at his wife and, before she could respond, he said, "We can go get it done before your Dad gets here. In fact, I will take all of you kids to get your haircut and done. Your Dad is not going to be in until the afternoon so we will get it all done in the morning."

Savannah wanted to tell Jonathan that the beauty shops don't open up that early, but she did not want to ruin the moment. Her husband did not want her to have to worry about it, so he was taking care of it and she was going to let him. She loved the way he was so attentive to her. It made her love him even more. However, he had taken it up a notch ever since they got the call about Mama.

Savannah looked at her husband and son, she loved them so much. Dominick was the spitting image of his father and she loved him too. If he turned out to be the same kind of man as his father that would be wonderful. She was not alone. She had her man and her son. She admitted to herself, *"God did not leave me alone. Yes, I know that, but I still need my mother."* Her thoughts battled each other. *"Lord why did you take her from me and why did she lie to me all these years? I can never forgive her for that."*

Dominick noticed his mother's face. Even at the age of two, he knew that he could make his mother happy. He learned the art of manipulation and he used it to see his mother smile. He knew that when he was in trouble all he had to do was say he was sorry and that he would behave. He did not know what the words meant, but he would repeat the phrase and his mother was no longer mad at him.

Dominick walked up to his mother and looked her in the eyes and said, "I sorry. I behave."

Savannah was so deep in thought that she just looked at her son. Not getting the usual response, the little boy did not know what to do. So, he repeated the statement.

"Mommy, I sorry. I behave."

Savannah smiled at her son and picked him up. She hugged him. "I love you."

Dominick responded, "I know dat."

She held her son and the love God had given her she gave to this little gift. He was truly a gift from God and she felt privileged to be his mother.

"Okay, let's all get into bed," Jonathan suggested yawning.

"Can we watch TV some more?" Tasha asked.

Well, yes, I guess. It's still early for you guys. But you two come with me," he said looking at Dominick and Da'Shawn. "It's time for you to go to bed."

Now best friends, they went in the room and got in the bed with no fuss. Jonathan had to come in once to tell them to stop talking and go to sleep. The other children lay down on a blanket in the living room until just after 10 when they all fell asleep. Jonathan helped them up and into their beds.

Jonathan and Savannah sat in the study looking through some of the bereavement cards and letters they received since it was quiet in the house. Jonathan looked at his wife and she was not the woman he knew. Understandably, she was grief-stricken, but there was more. He had never really seen

Savannah mad before. He knew she got upset like anyone else, especially with her boss, but this was different. Normally she was good-natured and always wanted to see the best out of the situation. Now Savannah was slipping away into a state of depression. Jonathan thought, *"Lord I know it has only been a few days but please help my baby forgive her mother and let her go."*

"Savannah, why don't you get some rest now?" Jonathan suggested.

"No, I'm not really tired. You guys let me sleep so I'm good. I want to get back to mom's journals. Maybe they will give me some idea why she did this to me."

"Baby, don't be like that. She didn't do anything bad to you. Your father and mother provided for you and Dominick and they died. You can't blame them for dying."

"I hear what you are saying, but I just can't get past the fact that my mother did not tell me all of this before she died. Jonathan, why would she lie to me? Would you do this to Dominick? I know I never would."

"No, Savannah, I would not have handled things the same way, but you cannot judge your parents by what you or I would have done. Good or bad, our parents did the best job they could and what you have to consider when looking at their actions is did they do it out of love. Did your mom and dad love you?" Jonathan asked. He did not wait for her to respond. "Yes, you know they did. So, if you know they were operating out of love for you, then you have to assume that what they did they thought was the best thing for you."

Allowing the Holy Spirit to speak through him, Jonathan continued. "Both of your parents were believers, so you have to know that God directed their paths. I don't mean to be harsh, sweetie, but you have to stop this. There are some simple truths that you have to just accept. Your mom is gone. She loved you. She left you a lot of money, and for whatever reason, she did not want you to know about it beforehand." He let his words hang in the air. He waited for her to respond, but she didn't; she just sat with her eyes closed. "*Lord, please speak to my wife,*" Jonathan prayed and then left the room.

Savannah sat in the small study with her eyes closed. There was nothing to say so she waited for God to speak to her. The ache in her heart had not dulled, but she could not cry any more. "*Lord,*" she started, but could not think of the words to say. She remembered her mother told her to pray in the Spirit when she did not know what to pray. She opened her mouth and words just spilled out. This foreign language sounded like Spanish and Italian, but she did not worry about that. She just let her mind flow from thought to thought and let the words flow.

The four angelic beings encompassed her and once again flapped their wings. The music that was created could not be heard, but Savannah began to sing in tongues. The glory of the Lord filled the house as it fell from heaven like rain. Marcus reached out with the permission of the Holy Spirit and touched Savannah's eyes. The touch allowed her to see more clearly into the spiritual realm. She could see the rain. She could see its orange glow. With her eyes still physically closed she could see the angels standing around her. As she watched them, she drifted off to sleep.

Chapter 11

Savannah woke to the smell of bacon and the noise of the children up and about. She thought about all that she had seen and heard last night. She decided it was all a dream and she would keep it to herself. The last thing she wanted to do was worry Jonathan any more than she already had. Slowly, she lifted herself out of the leather chair and onto her feet. As she made her way to the kitchen, she caught the eye of Dominick before she could get there.

"Mommy, Mommy!" he said as he ran to her.

"Hey, sweetie," Savannah said as she picked her son up.

"Babe, you hungry?" Jonathan asked as Savannah walked into the kitchen.

"Yes I am. That all smells so good!"

Jonathan fixed his wife a plate of bacon, eggs and pancakes. He was so glad she was going to eat that he put a little extra on. He lovingly gave her instructions to finish it all while he was gone with the kids to get their hair done. Everyone was just about finished eating their breakfast and ready to go. The excitement of the children was palpable. Even Dominick was excited to go to the barbershop although he had been a couple of times with his father.

"What shop are you going to?" Savannah asked.

Jonathan answered, "We are just going to drive around until we find a barbershop and beauty shop open near each other."

"Okay," Savannah said, "but here take my card."

Savannah ran back to the study and got the new banking card she got from Freedom Bank and gave it to Jonathan.

"Just get cash out. Don't try and use it at the shops," she instructed. "You're cute, but you don't look like me at all." Savannah snickered.

Jonathan smiled. He was starting to see the old Savannah coming back. With a kiss and a hug Jonathan and the children were out the door.

Savannah sat looking at her food and decided to eat it all knowing that she would be questioned later as to its disposition. As she sat alone in her mother's house, she ate and prayed to God to take away her hurt and pain. She asked God to forgive her for her anger and resentment towards her mother. She asked her mother to forgive her as well. She had no clue if her mother could even hear her after death, but she spoke the words anyway. As she ate her food, she thought about her mother and all that she had done for her growing up and now. She still did not understand why her mother did what she did, but she was better with it now.

Savannah finished her food and cleaned up the mess that was in the kitchen. She loved when Jonathan cooked, but he made a mess when he did. As she cleaned, she thought about how her life had changed.

"No more bills!" she said out loud. "No more of that stupid job and no more of that idiot, Robert King! Whoa, thank you, Jesus and thank you, Mama." As she wiped the counters and stove, she could feel some of her pain being taken away.

She decided that she needed to pack up her mother's things. She looked around the room and decided against it. She had gained a lot of ground emotionally the last few days, but not enough yet to go through all of her mother's things. Jonathan and Estella could help her with it later. So, she went back to the study where she found solace and back to her mother's journals. She sat down in the leather chair and prayed.

Savannah prayed. "Lord, please help me get through this. I don't really know where to go or what to do."

She waited to hear or feel something. She sat still and tried to concentrate. She cried, "God, please . . ." but she heard nothing still. She started to get angry again. Just then, in the spiritual realm, a tiny crack appeared in her countenance. The demons of Anger and Unforgiveness appeared in the room. Both demons were strongholds and needed only the tiniest opening to appear.

Anger spoke to her first. "Your mother lied to you. You have every right to be angry. You can't ever forgive her for that."

Unforgiveness added.

The pair took turns speaking to her. In the spiritual realm, the words formed a yellow cloud around her. It weighed her down and she started to feel angry once again.

Marcus stood back and just watched, he knew that Savannah would have to give him permission to fight on her behalf with her prayers. She would have to use the weapons God had given His children to fight off the attack of the enemy. The demons could feel their influence taking hold. It was critical that they kept talking while they had her attention. They had successfully stopped her from praying. They just needed to keep her distracted. This was a critical time. If done correctly they could not only affect her, but also everyone connected to Savannah. Anger looked at his subject and lusted to devour her and her happy little life. He planned to first take her down then her marriage then her son. Unforgiveness planned to follow Anger and seal the deal. He would ensure that this incident was passed down through the family line. He intended to produce a generational curse. The pair was simply giddy at the possibilities.

Anger and Unforgiveness worked side-by-side most of the time. They found the partnership to be very beneficial. With just a glance from Unforgiveness, the plan was set into motion. The two stood looking at Marcus and laughed. Marcus stood patiently waiting for instructions. Savannah sat under the influence of the demonic presence in the room. Her fury grew until it was palpable. With no immediate target to direct the fury, Anger needled Savannah.

"Rose should have never left those kids for you to take care of. She is a terrible mother. She's just a worthless junkie. You need to tell her how you feel. She needs to know that you don't treat children that way. Everyone is afraid of her, but you need to stand up to her and tell her how bad she is". As the words came out of the demon's mouth the cloud got thicker.

While Jonathan and the kids were out, Brian called Jonathan.

"Hey, Jonathan," Brian said, "I was so excited about picking up the kids I went to the airport early. I was able to go standby on another flight. I am here. I just landed a few minutes ago."

"Oh, okay. Um . . . well," Jonathan explained, "My son Dominick, and Da'Shawn got Tasha's hair wet and we were going to get it done then the boys wanted to get a haircut so we are at the barbershop now. The boys are finished, but Tasha is not. Hold on Brian." Jonathan asked the hairdresser how much longer it would take to finish Tasha's hair. She told him it would be another thirty minutes. He got back on the phone with Brian. "Man, it's going to be another thirty minutes here. I don't know how long it takes to get to the airport from here. I want to go pick up my wife first. I know she will want to come. It may be a little while before we get there," Jonathan said.

"That is fine. I will be here. I need to eat some lunch anyway," Brian replied.

"Okay, great. I will call you when we are on our way, Brian."

"Okay. See you when you get here."

Jonathan called Savannah to apprise her of the situation. Before Jonathan could say anything else she said, "Come back and get me before you go".

"That is what I was planning to do, sweetie. Tasha only has thirty minutes left so we will come back to the house and get you and the kids' luggage shortly. We are right around the corner from the KFC we went to."

"Alright, I'll be ready," Savannah said, then hung up the phone. She jumped up out of the chair and headed to the bathroom to get ready.

As Savannah walked into the bathroom, Holy Spirit spoke to her. *"Rose needs your prayers. She needs you. Pray for her."*

"That's a joke right, God?" she answered back. "I have no intention of praying for that bitch." Savannah stopped, blinked her eyes and shook her head at her own words. It was not like her to swear. *"Wow, girl, get a grip,"* she told herself.

Anger spoke quickly. "But she is a bitch. Look at what she did to you and those kids."

"All that money she stole from you," Unforgiveness added. The pair continued the onslaught until Jonathan arrived to pick her up.

When Savannah got into the car Jonathan noticed the expression on his wife's face but said nothing. As they drove to the airport, the children were ecstatic. The children bounced with anticipation as they drove down the interstate towards the airport. The children were talking about everything they were going to tell their father and what they were going to do when they got back to Chicago. In the midst of it all, Savannah overheard Tasha say but what about mama? With that question, the children all fell silent.

Savannah said, "Why do you care about her? After all she abandoned you guys."

A stunned Jonathan shot a look at Savannah. "What? I can't believe you just said that!"

"It's the truth," she said. Not wanting to discuss it in front of the children Jonathan held his peace.

As Jonathan drove he asked God what to do. "*Pray for your wife. She is being attacked.*" he heard in his spirit. Jonathan immediately began to pray for Savannah. For the remainder of the trip Jonathan said nothing. After realizing the harshness of her words, Savannah tried to change the subject.

"Are you excited to fly on a plane?"

"What do you mean?" they asked consecutively.

"You are going to fly back tomorrow with your dad."

The questions just flew back and forth.

"Wait, I thought we told you. We got you guys tickets to go back with your dad."

When they arrived at the airport, Jonathan was lucky enough to find a parking space near the entrance. They climbed out and went inside. The kids' heads were on a swivel as they gawked with their mouths open. They had not been to an airport before. Even Dominick was fascinated. Jonathan and Savannah had to hold their hands to keep them moving until they reached the baggage claim area.

Brian looked nothing like what Savannah thought he would. Standing in front of the bank of three escalators, she watched as he came up the center escalator to face them. Tasha screamed Daddy so loud that everyone around turned to look at him. He was very tall, about 6'5", dark-skinned and very big. He was not fat, but very big nonetheless. He looked like a professional football player. Despite his intimidating stature, his smile was very inviting. His teeth seemed like they were painted white and you could see all of them when he smiled. As he walked towards the children, the three older ones ran towards him while the Da'Shawn stayed back a little ways. In one swoop, he dropped his suitcase and picked up all three children. He held them and they hugged him in the middle of the hall in front of the escalators.

"Let's get out of the way here," Jonathan said as the people behind tried to get around the reunited family. Brian squeezed the children once more and dropped them and took his suitcase from Jonathan. After taking the case he extended his free hand to shake Jonathan's hand.

"Brian Jackson," he said in a deep baritone voice.

Jonathan grabbed his hand and said, "Jonathan Miller. Nice to meet you in person." Jonathan turned to Savannah. "This is Savannah, my wife, and our son, Dominick."

Brian stepped forward and hugged Savannah. "It is so nice to meet you."

"Likewise," Savannah said.

Brian stooped down to Dominick and looked him in the eye. "It's nice to meet you too, sir."

Dominick smiled, but hid behind his mother's leg.

"Did you check anything?" Jonathan asked.

"No. I just have this overnight bag. I just want to get my kids and get home. My wife and I have waited so long for this I can't even tell you. Thank you so much for helping them."

"It was no problem at all," Savannah said. "They are family, so you are too. Let's get you to the hotel so you can rest.

"I am not tired at all. I just want to spend time with my children," Brian said with a huge grin.

They all climbed into the van. The children insisted that Brian sit with them. He got in and had to sit at an angle in order to accommodate his legs. The van was abuzz with the children and Brian making plans and catching up.

Savannah interrupted. "Brian, we booked you and the kids a room at the hotel that we put the kids and Rose in when they got here. They have a free breakfast buffet so you guys can eat a good breakfast before you get on the plane."

"Oh, that sounds great!" he said.

As they drove to the hotel, the heavenly quartet assigned to the Millers was joined by another angel. This angel traveled with Brian and moved in sync with the others silently around the van. Along the way Marcus nudged the car in the next lane as it drifted. The driver was reading a text and not paying attention. With the brush of his wing, the driver was back in the correct lane. Startled at the sight of the van beside him, the driver decided to put the phone down. Yet another instance when God's warriors protected his children from the unseen dangers.

Savannah had called ahead and secured a suite for them knowing the children would not want to be separated from Brian. After all everyone's luggage was put into the room, Brian and the kids met the Millers downstairs for an early dinner.

"Maybe we can just talk for awhile. I am not really hungry. I got something at the airport while I waited for you guys to get there,"

Well, let's take the kids somewhere where they can have some fun," Jonathan suggested.

"That sounds great to me," Brian said.

Savannah did a quick search on her phone. She announced, "I found the perfect place. It's a restaurant and arcade called Wave. The kids can play while we talk. Oh, they also have Karaoke if you want to, Brian.

"No, no! I can't sing a lick," he laughed.

"Oh. Okay, well it should be fun for the kids anyway."

Wave turned out to be a really neat place. It was a combination of a restaurant, arcade, and bar. When they walked through the doors, the atmosphere was of an old English pub like the ones in the movies. The lighting was dim and there was a lot of dark wood. There were benches to sit on while waiting but it wasn't crowded. They moved to the restaurant and arcade area, which was lit more brightly. The arcade area was just beyond the restaurant and Savannah could see the flashing lights of the games. She also heard the games and was glad that the hostess sat them a little further away so they could talk without having to yell. The large room was filled with families and lots of children. Savannah looked around the room and at the dishes some were eating to determine if she could figure out what she wanted. She always did this when she was visiting a new restaurant. She spotted a table where a gentleman was eating a salmon dish. It looked quite good and Savannah decided that's what she was going to order.

Jonathan took the menu and decided on a steak dinner with all the trimmings. The children chose between a corndog, macaroni and cheese, chicken fingers, or hamburger with fries.

Jonathan asked, "Brian, are you sure you don't want to get something to eat to take back to the hotel?"

"Yeah, maybe I will order something." Brian settled on a hamburger and fries. "This will probably hold up better in the microwave back of the room."

As everyone ate, the adults engaged in small talk while the children quickly gobbled up their food as soon as their plates were placed on the table. They wanted to get to the arcade as soon as possible. When the children finished eating Tasha looked at Brian pleading to be let loose from the restraints of the table. Following her lead the rest of the children whined and begged as well.

Before Brian could say anything, Jonathan stood up and said, "I got them."

The kids yelled yay and scooted their chairs back. Within a few seconds they made their way through the restaurant and were standing at the entrance of the arcade waiting for Jonathan who was moving way too slow.

Brian smiled. "I guess I will have all the time in the world now to spend with them." He spoke so earnestly to Savannah that she wanted to cry. "Thank you so much for taking care of my kids." Savannah watched Brian looking at the children disappearing into the arcade.

"It's our pleasure," she said. "I'm glad we had a chance to spend time with them because my mother and Rose did not get along. I didn't know the kids that well. Well, truth be told, I only remembered Tasha. It's a shame that it takes a wedding or a funeral for a family to come together."

"Yeah, you're right. Unfortunately, that's the way it is sometimes." Brian said.

Marcus and the other angels took their positions around the building. So much light emanated from them that the building was much brighter than normal. Although human eyes could not physically see them, their effect was felt. As long as they were there, the demons inside the building, and there were many, could not harm the group.

After following the group to the restaurant, Anger and Unforgiveness took their places behind Savannah and whispered in her ear. She was the only one who had a door open for them. They had tried and failed with Brian and his wife a long time ago, so they had moved on to Rose and the children. The children, however, were not yet of age so their influence was stifled by God's protection. Children could not hold a grudge for long as God had intended for all of his children.

With Savannah so angry, they had another opportunity to destroy this family. Rose was theirs, but they could not seem to get her children because of Brian and his wife's prayers for God's protection to cover them.

However, this did not stop them from constantly trying. If they could not use the Rose's children, they would use anyone they could exert influence over, anyone open to their suggestions, to destroy this family for suggestions were all they could use. They could not make anyone do anything. Nevertheless, they set about their task eagerly. This family was no different than any other. God's enemy seemed to pay close attention to those that received extra angelic protection.

As they sat at the table, Savannah's mind started to wander back to the children. She thought about how Rose treated not only the children but her as well. She hadn't spent a whole lot of time with Rose. But she knew that her mother and Rose did not have a close relationship. She often wondered in these situations how God expected her to love someone so hateful.

Normally, Savannah thought the best of people. Until she was proven otherwise, she expected others to act with civility. She had not encountered very many people like Rose in her life, so she wasn't quite sure how to react to her. However, she did know she didn't like her despite the fact that she was her aunt. Savannah began to get angry and started entertaining the thoughts and suggestions from the demonic forces around her.

Savannah looked Brian in the eye. "I don't know how in the world you've dealt with Rose for this long. She's an awful human being and she needs to be locked up. What she did to those kids is unforgivable. I can't even imagine what she's been into. How could she just leave the children by themselves? It is beyond me how a mother could treat her children like that. I just hate her." Savannah frowned in disgust.

Brian looked at her astonished. "Why would you say something like that? She needs our help and prayers. How could you hate her? She's your aunt and really, she didn't do anything to you, per say. She did to me and the kids. You can't live your life like that hating people. That's not godly at all. Truth be told, God wants her soul just as much as yours or mine. God never gave up on us and we cannot give up on her. My wife and I continue to pray for her and ask God to draw her in because He truly wants her for Himself. If we give up on her then who will she have to pray for her? What she is dealing with are some strong demons. The kinds that Jesus said come out only through fasting and prayer."

Savannah sat thinking about what Brian had just said and realized that he was telling the truth. She felt terrible and realized that God was speaking to her through Brian. She silently prayed and asked God to forgive her.

With their grip on Savannah loosened, Anger and Unforgiveness quickly recovered and decided to focus on Rose and left for the moment. They planned to attempt to influence her at another time.

"God forgave you, so you have to forgive her," Brian declared. "I had to learn that and am continuing to learn this daily. She has done so much to me and my wife that you would not even believe."

"Like what?" Savannah asked.

"Oh, that's not important. My point is that you can't let what she has done change who you are."

Tasha ran to the table and said, "Daddy, come play with us!"

"Okay!"

Brian got up and followed Tasha leaving Savannah sitting and thinking at the table. *"Lord, I know what he said is true, but it's so hard not to be angry with her. I need you to help me with that."* Savannah took a drink of water then joined the rest of the bunch in the arcade. They played and had fun until the children were all worn out.

Back at the hotel, Brian told Tasha to take the kids up to the room to get ready for bed. Dominick wanted to go with them as well.

Jonathan said, "Okay, but don't get Tasha's hair wet again."

Tasha exclaimed, "No way! They can take a bath without me!"

Da'Shawn and Dominick glanced at each other and laughed. "They ain't gonna mess up my hair again!"

Jonathan said to Dominick, "You don't need to take a bath here. You will take one when we get back to the house. Just play with your cousins until we get finished."

"Okay," Dominick sang as he turned around in a circle.

"Somebody's tired," Savannah said looking at her son.

"I not tired," protested Dominick as he stopped to look at his mother.

"Okay, little man, whatever you say."

"We won't be long, Tasha," Brian stated.

"Okay, Daddy."

The adults followed the children up to the suite. Brian shook his head and sat on the sofa in the living room area. "I am so grateful to God and you for calling me. We have prayed so long to have them come and stay with us," he said quietly. "The court would not let them because Rose told the court that I sexually abused Tasha when she was little and that my wife physically abused them."

"Oh my goodness! What happened?" Savannah gasped.

"There was no evidence of any abuse, but the investigation alone was devastating to both of us. When that didn't work, she claimed that the kids were not mine. We had to get DNA tests on them. It was only when all three came back as my children that she stopped saying they weren't mine. She has conned us out of so much money that when she told me about Bertha, I did not believe her. I've learned not to give her money, but to buy whatever the kids needed. I have to show the court my receipts every month. I checked to make sure that everything she was saying was the truth, so I made some inquiries first. When I found out Bertha had passed, I purchased the bus tickets. We kept praying that one day she will come around and see that my wife and I just want the best for all the children, not just my three. My wife keeps telling me not to stop doing things for the kids and to remember that God knows everything and that He will fix it all. If it wasn't for her, I would have given up long ago. She is an amazing woman." He let his words trail off and he stared off into the distance for a few moments.

He continued. "She has put up with a lot from Rose. Rose has said so many hurtful things to her, but my baby still prays for her and wants to have all the children come stay with us anyway. It's so weird. We have been praying the same prayer for so long it feels strange to have it come true. That sounds strange, but this all feels surreal to me and I just want to get home with my kids. I will deal with the courts later, but right now, this is an answered prayer." He leaned back into the sofa and Savannah saw tears welling up in Brian's eyes. He sighed, "It has been such a hard road with all of this. My wife and I have tried to have children of our own, but we lost two when my wife was in her second trimester for both. It was devastating. I believe it was the stress behind all of what Rose was doing that caused it."

"Oh, I am so sorry!" Savannah said.

"How in the world did you get through it?" Jonathan asked.

"It was only through our relationship with God that did it. We prayed and cried, but in the end, we knew that He was in control of it all. Now don't get me wrong. I was very mad, and all of this did not happen overnight. There were many days that I thought I could not make it. I even thought about having someone take Rose out." That comment drew raised eyebrows from both Jonathan and Savannah. "Oh, don't let my demeanor and conversation today fool you. I am from the south side of Chicago. I grew up in one of the worst neighborhoods ever. I know some people that it would just take one call from me and she would have been history." He paused and then said, "But God!"

He shook his head and closed his eyes at that. Not wanting to disturb him they remained quiet. Jonathan and Savannah just looked at Brian then at each other. After a few more moments, Brian looked up and said, "God sure is good."

"Yes, He is!" Jonathan agreed.

Savannah stood. "It is getting late. We better let you get to bed and get Dominick home."

"Oh, okay," Brian said. "It was so nice to meet both of you. Maybe you can come to Chicago to spend time with the family."

"That would be great," Savannah said, feeling a real connection with him. "We want to check up on the kids too so maybe in a few months, okay?"

"That sounds fine. I will let my wife know. I am sure she will be very excited to meet you both."

"We want to say goodbye to the kids now, but we will take you guys to the airport tomorrow."

Brian waved his hand. "Oh, that is not necessary. The hotel has a shuttle. The front desk told me yesterday when I checked in."

"Okay. When do you leave?" Jonathan asked since he did not purchase the tickets.

"The flight leaves at about 1p.m. so if we leave here at ten, I think that would give us enough time."

"Okay. Well, we will meet you here, at say eight, for breakfast. Is that okay?" Savannah said.

Brian nodded. "That sounds good."

They rose and walked to the bedroom and found the kids asleep on the floor; only Tasha was awake watching TV. Jonathan grabbed Dominick and they headed to the van.

In the car, Savannah said, "I want to give Brian and his wife something to help out."

"I was thinking the same thing. But how do we do it and not insult them or make them feel like they will owe us later?" Savannah pondered.

"Well, first I think we need to give it for the kids. I don't think they would refuse it," he said glancing at his wife.

"You are right. We can tell him it's for college for all of them."

"How much do you think is enough?"

Savannah sighed as she gazed out the passenger window. "I don't know. Let's pray on it tonight and see what the Lord says in the morning."

"Works for me," Jonathan agreed as they pulled into the driveway.

After putting Dominick down in the guest bedroom, Jonathan grabbed Savannah's hand and pulled her close to him. He said nothing, but silently prayed for his wife. After a while, he let her go and kissed her on her forehead.

"I love you baby and I know it has been very hard on you, but I just want you to know that I am here for you to lean on. I am praying for you too. You are not alone."

Savannah stepped back and looked at Jonathan. He was saying the same words she said to herself when she prayed. Joy filled her heart for the first time since she got the call about her mother.

Chapter 12

Anger and Unforgiveness were hovering about waiting for a chance to influence Savannah again but the joy Savannah was feeling was so overpowering that they could not stand in the midst of it and they left. Not completely deterred, Unforgiveness moved off just outside the house, just far enough to watch, but not close enough to engage the four angels. Anger conferred with his compatriot and they both decided it was too much trouble for that time being and they would return later when another opportunity presented or could be manufactured for them to interject.

After a hot shower Jonathan and Savannah went and sat on the bed in the master bedroom.

Jonathan asked, "Savannah, do you feel weird about sleeping in your mother's bed?"

"I did at first when I got here, but not now. I feel like she is still here, but not in a creepy way."

"Are you still angry with her?"

"No, not at the moment. I have been thinking about what you said and I know she loved me so I'm trying to let the anger go, my aunt is another story. Why do you ask?"

"Just so I know how to pray for you," Jonathan said as he grabbed his wife's hand. "Let's pray."

Following her husband's lead, she prayed for the children, Brian and his wife, and Estella and Raul. She spoke blessings over them all and ended with a prayer and blessing over her own family in Jesus' name.

At the name of Jesus, even the distance that Anger and Unforgiveness had moved from the house was not enough. They shrieked with pain and slithered into the darkness.

Jonathan prayed in agreement with all his wife spoke and also said a prayer for Rose and Savannah. He prayed that forgiveness and love would rule their actions towards Rose. He also spoke blessing over everyone and ended the prayer in Jesus' name.

The following morning, they met Brian and the children at the hotel for breakfast. The kids were so excited about the new life they were starting. No one even mentioned Rose, which struck Savannah as strange.

"What will happen when Rose shows up at your house?" Savannah whispered to Brian.

"Well, we will see, but I don't think I will have any problem getting custody of them now.

If I have to go to court will you two testify and tell what happened?"

"Of course, whatever you need, man," Jonathan asserted. "We wanted to give you something for the kids to help out with their college and all."

Jonathan looked at Savannah and she pulled a check out of her purse for five hundred thousand dollars. Brian stared at the check and blinked his eyes and mouthed the amount to make sure it was real. Then he said the amount out loud and gazed at them.

"Are you serious?" he uttered in shock.

"Yes." Savannah smiled. "My mother left me an inheritance and I want to make sure my cousins are taken care of. Use it however you see fit. Just make sure that they have what they need, please."

"Oh, thank you, Jesus!" Brian exclaimed with tears rolling down his face. "I don't know what to say."

"You said it right the first time — thank you, Jesus. God has blessed us, and I know that we are supposed to bless others," Savannah said. They hugged each other.

Jonathan nodded. "Just take care of your family man, and God will do the rest. He's got your back."

Brian just shook his head again and said, "I need to call my wife. She is not going to believe this."

"Okay, but we need to get you guys on the plane," Savannah warned looking at the time on her phone.

"Yes, you are right," Brian said. "I can tell her once we land in Chicago. She will be picking us up anyway."

Da'Shawn and Dominick were holding hands and Dominick tried to get in the hotel van with them, but Jonathan grabbed the little boy's hand.

"No, little man. You are staying with us."

Dominick shrieked, "No! Want to go" and started crying, which made everyone laugh and cry. They said their goodbyes and they were off.

Jonathan buckled Dominick, now hysterical, into his car seat. After a few minutes, the little boy was silently looking out the window as they drove. On the way back to the house, Savannah pondered, "What do you think we should do about the house?"

Jonathan knew when Savannah asked a question, she had been thinking about it already, so he simply said, "I don't know. What do you want to do with it?"

"Well, we don't need it and if we sell it, then what? It seems like we should do something special in memory of Mama."

"What were you thinking?" Jonathan asked.

"Well, what would you say if I said let's give it to Estella? She is living in that old folks home and that can't be that good."

"Um," was all Jonathan said while Savannah revealed the remainder of her thoughts. She went on about how Estella was mama's best friend and mama would probably want me to do something for her.

Finally, Jonathan said, "If that is what you want to do, then call Estella and see if she can come by the house."

"Well she will probably have to wait on Raul, but I will call." Savannah dialed the number and told Estella that she wanted to talk to her and asked could she come by.

"Sure, sweetie. Is everything all right?"

"Yes, everything is fine. We just want to talk to you about something."

"Okay. I call Raul and . . ." Then Estella started to yell in Spanish to someone in the distance. She came back to the phone. "Okay, querida. I see you later." While Savannah was saying goodbye, she heard Estella go off again with a string of Spanish words and then the phone was dead.

"Okay," Savannah said with a sigh, "Guess she is coming later."

Savannah thought about Estella and her mother and thought what an odd pair they were. She smiled and said out loud, "I will have to find out the story of how they met."

"Who are you talking about, baby?" Jonathan asked. "Your mom and Estella?"

"Yeah when I think about it, they don't seem like they would be friends at all. Estella is so sweet, but she is so feisty and Momma is kinda laid back." Savannah caught herself using the present tense for her mom and she felt a sob rise in her throat.

After a few seconds Dominick spoke. He was watching his mother and saw the tear fall from her eyes. "Don't be sad, Mommy. Why you cry, Mommy?"

"I'm okay, baby. I just miss Nannie."

"Nannie okay, Mommy, da good birds took her with dem."

Savannah said, "Okay, sweetie I know. I just miss her."

"Okay, Mommy, but don't cry. I behave. Don't cry, Mommy."

The thought of her son trying to comfort her the best way he knew how was so reassuring to her. She was so blessed to have both of her men in her life.

Jonathan whispered to Savannah, "He keeps talking about birds, good ones and bad ones. What do you think he means?"

"I don't know. He's so little he probably heard it on TV or something," Savannah answered.

Just then, Dominick started singing *Twinkle, Twinkle Little Star*, then *Elmo's World*, then *Jesus Loves Me*. After he kept saying "lubs me" instead of "loves me", both Savannah and Jonathan were smiling. All three sang together all the way back to the house.

Chapter 13

"We need to think about getting back to our home," Jonathan announced. "I know I just have to get myself together to go back to that job."

"You know you don't have to go back."

"I don't mean to work. I just mean to get my stuff and really say goodbye to Jean and everybody."

Savannah moaned. "I know Robert is going to have something to say and I just want to avoid him altogether."

"Do you want me to go with you?" offered Jonathan.

"Yes! I would like you to be with me. That would be great. You could get my stuff while I say goodbye and see human resources."

"Doesn't it feel good to know that you can just quit?"

"Yes but knowing Robert I am already fired." They both burst into laughter.

"We need to pack up mom's stuff we are going to take back with us," Jonathan suggested.

"I really only want the personal stuff and the clock I bought her. The rest of this can be donated or if Estella takes the house, she can keep it. I hope she does. I really don't want to sell Mama's house."

"I'm sure she will take it," Jonathan said. "It has to be better than living in that home."

Savannah grabbed a photo album and sat down in the living room. She started looking through the old photos of her family. Dominick walked up to his mother and she pulled him onto her lap and showed him the pictures of when she was a child. Savannah thanked God for her parents and her own family then kissed her sweet Dominick.

"Mommy loves you."

"I know dat," he responded, and she hugged him tightly. Soon Dominick got bored with the pictures and squirmed to get down.

After an hour of sorting she had only gotten through old pictures and kitchen stuff. Savannah said exasperated, "This is just too much to do all at once."

Jonathan suggested, "Baby, let's just call a moving company to pack up what we are going to take back with us. All you would have to do is just tell them and me what you want." Before Savannah could answer Jonathan added, "I will call one to come tomorrow."

"Thank you so much, honey. I would have never thought of that, you are so smart. I am so lucky to have you."

At the praise Jonathan just beamed. Even after so long together, Savannah could still make him feel so good.

"No, I'm lucky to have you," he smiled as he kissed her forehead then left the room with Dominick trailing him.

"It's about time for his nap," Savannah yelled down the hall.

Dominick yelled back, "I not tired" and ran back to Savannah. "I not tired, Mommy."

"I know, baby, but you need a nap so that you can grow. Remember I told you that you grow when you are sleeping?"

"Yesh," he said as tears formed in his eyes.

"You want to grow up to be a big man like Daddy, right?"

"Yesh," the little boy responded.

"Okay then, let's go take a nap."

"I hungry," he murmured.

"You can have something to eat when you get up from your nap."

Seeing that there was no getting out of a nap, Dominick relented and followed Savannah down the hall to the guest room. He climbed into bed. Putting him in the bed with its stiff starched sheets reminded her of when she was a little girl and her mother tucked her in so tight she could hardly move. Why her mother insisted on starching and ironing the bed sheets was beyond her and she did not pick up the practice. She recalled, as she kissed Dominick's cheek, how she would have to press them when she got older and swore when she had her own kids, she would never subject them to that kind of abuse. She shook her head and shut the door as she walked out. The trip into her past was interrupted when a car pulled into the drive. Jonathan looked out of the window of the study and turned to Savannah as she walked past.

"Estella and Raul are here," he said.

After a long hug, Estella waved to Raul and he left. "He wants to see his girlfriend," she said. Savannah waved and they proceeded to the couch.

"Jonathan, can you come in here?" Savannah called.

"Where is that baby?" Estella asked.

"I just put him down for a nap."

"Oh, shoot well, I won't wake him up then."

As Jonathan joined them, Savannah grabbed Estella's hand. "We want to do something for you. We have been talking about it and we want to give you Momma's house. It's paid off so you could live here mortgage and rent-free. I know that those retirement communities are expensive so this would help you out, right?" Savannah looked at Estella and when she was strangely silent, she then focused on Jonathan. Estella waited to speak a few moments longer than expected and Savannah did not know what to do. "I didn't mean to insult you. We just thought you would take care of the house like my Mama would have."

Estella finally spoke. "You are truly your mother's child. Your mom said you would do this."

"What? How could she know?"

"You and your mother think alike. She asked me to come live with her a few months ago with the hopes of me keeping the house when she was gone, but I told her that it belonged to you. I so appreciate the offer, but I cannot live here. Your mom was my best friend for many years. This house holds too many memories for me. Besides that, all my friends at Sunnyvale. I would have no one to pick me up to go see them when I want to. Niña," she said as she looked at Savannah, "at my age I need to be around the same stuff and same people. I don't like no change too much."

Savannah looked at Jonathan who just shrugged and said, "Okay then. I guess we can sell it."

Estella suggested, "Why don't you keep it for now? Maybe you can sell it later, but I can come by and check on it now and then. I still have a key."

Jonathan said, "Yeah, baby, we don't have to decide everything now. Let's let a few months pass and then see what we want to do when things are not so fresh."

"I guess so," Savannah said.

"I know you have a mental list of the stuff you want to check off, but let things simmer down first," said Jonathan.

Recognizing her habit of trying to order chaos by checking things off a list, she relented. They sat and talked until Raul came back an hour later and took Estella back to the retirement home.

Chapter 14

Jonathan walked back to check on Dominick. He was still asleep. Just then another car pulled into the driveway.

"It's Rose," he told Savannah.

Through the study window, he watched Rose get out of the car. He studied the driver's side window but could not see through the tinted glass. The driver remained in the car with it running. Rose rang the doorbell.

As soon as Savannah opened the door, Rose shouted, "Where is Tasha? I'm taking her with me!

"Your children are not here," Savannah said calmly.

"Where are they? Tasha needs to come with me right now!"

"Brian came and picked them up this morning because we could not get a hold of you."

"What do you mean Brian picked them up? I have custody of them. He can't just pick them up."

Savannah stated, "When we could not get in touch with you, we called him. You left them in a hotel all by themselves. Where the heck were you anyway?"

As Savannah asked that question, Anger, who was watching from a distance, stepped closer to the pair. He spoke in the ears of both planting thoughts and suggestions. He told Rose that she had no right judging her. She is supposed to be so damned perfect, she ain't nothing but a hypocrite like her stank ass mama! He told Savannah that she was a terrible mother and person. He said she is a thief and a crackhead. Those kids are better off without her. Why doesn't she just let their father have them, they will be better off. His exact words were repeated by both Rose and Savannah. As the argument progressed both women were getting more and more angry. The demon was getting more excited by the second. Hearing the elevation in his wife's voice, Jonathan stepped from around the corner to let Rose see him.

"Baby, is everything all right?" he asked.

Before Savannah could say anything Rose blurted out, "No, everything is not all right! I want to know where Tasha is." Rose did not yell at Jonathan. She spoke in a lower voice than she had spoken to Savannah.

"All the children are on a plane right now on their way back to Chicago. As Savannah has already told you," Jonathan explained calmly, "we could not reach you and we called

Brian to come and pick them up. They could not stay in the hotel by themselves, so we brought them back here. When you did not answer our calls, we had no choice but to call Brian. You need to be thankful we did not call the police. You would be in jail right now. Now since they are not here, you need to leave." Jonathan stepped in front of Savannah.

With that move Anger backed away staying away from the angel now looming over Jonathan. He moved to the top of the car and spoke, "Oh I'll leave, but I will be back. This is not over." Savannah looked and saw the darkness in Rose's face and the yellow tinge in her eyes. "*She is on something,*" she thought.

Jonathan closed the door, but before he went back to the study he kissed his wife and gave her a reassuring hug. They packed until Dominick woke up and was hungry. He climbed out of the bed and walked into the living room to Savannah. She was so engrossed in the pictures that she didn't hear him. When he put his little hand on her arm she was startled.

"Mommy, I hungry," he said.

"Okay, baby, I'll get you something to eat," she said as she kissed his chocolate-dimpled cheeks. She held his hand as they walked into the kitchen. While making him a sandwich, Savannah looked out the kitchen window and saw a bench swing.

"Nannie's got a swing. Do you want to go out there and eat with Mommy?" she asked.

"Yesh," the little boy said.

Savannah made two more turkey sandwiches and found some apple juice in the refrigerator. After pouring three glasses she took one sandwich and glass of juice to Jonathan in the study.

"We are going to eat in the backyard," she told him. "There is a swing back there and a huge magnolia tree."

"This swing doesn't surprise me. Mama loved magnolia blossoms," Savannah thought as they placed their drinks on the small table on the deck flanked by the matching chairs. "Let's eat here and then we can get on the swing," she told her son. As they ate, Savannah observed how manicured the lawn was. It definitely reflected the interior of the house. Her mother was meticulous in everything she did. She watched her son finish his sandwich and reach for the glass of juice. She knew what was going to happen if she did not intervene to help the little one.

She grabbed the glass and to help when he immediately said, "No, Mommy, I do it!"

"Okay, you can do it," she said, "but be careful."

As he lifted the glass to his mouth, the liquid spilled all over his front. Dominick looked to his mother expecting something. Juice was all over him and the cushions. Savannah said nothing, but just looked at her son and waited for him to ask for help. Not knowing what to do, the little boy started to cry.

"Do you want Mama to help now?"

"Yesh," he said with tears running down his cheeks.

Savannah took him into the house to clean him up and put him in fresh clothes. They ventured back to the swing.

Jonathan appeared at the back door. "Ya'll going to leave me inside to do all the work?"

Savannah smiled. "Come here, that can wait."

They sat on the swing in silence for a while. Savannah thought about all that had happened since she got the call about her mother at work. It seemed like so long ago, but in a short amount of time, her whole world had changed. Still grieving the loss of her mother, she could not really take in the enormity of her situation. She did not even want to think about the money and how it would change their lives. She would leave all of that to Jonathan.

Jonathan broke the silence. "I made reservations so we have only two more days to get everything settled before we go back."

"Okay," Savannah responded. "I guess we have to get back."

"You sound disappointed. I thought you were anxious to get home."

"I was at first, but now I don't know. I feel so close to Mama here. It's hard to think about leaving because then she will really be gone."

Jonathan didn't say anything. He just grabbed his wife's hand and silently prayed for her. He, too, was missing Bertha, but not like Savannah. They had been close and Bertha could always be counted on for insight about his wife. He recalled the times they had talked before the wedding and when Dominick was born. Bertha had been ecstatic on both occasions and he saw for the first time how similar Savannah and her mother were. He remembered how they would talk for hours and not complete a full sentence. One would start off with "do you remember when we went to that place," and the other would say, "yeah, that was so fun; we got to go back". He would try to join the conversation, but it took too long for them to explain everything so he just let them have their "coded language"; he would get the deciphered version from Savannah later. He had no clue what they were talking about, but somehow, they did. He always wondered if he would someday be in tune with Savannah in that way. He doubted it, but he knew that he and Savannah had their own special bond and that was enough for him. As long as he had her love, he thought they could do anything.

Bored of the silence, Dominick climbed down and ran in a circle in the yard. For some odd reason Dominick looked strange to her; there was something missing. Then it hit her.

She turned to Jonathan and asked, "Where is Spiderman?"

Jonathan said, "I don't know. Dominick, where is your Spiderman? We are going on the plane and I don't want to be looking for it at the last minute."

"I gave it to 'Shawn," he said without stopping.

Both Savannah and Jonathan looked at each other and then to their son. "You gave it to Da'Shawn?" they both asked.

"Yesh, he no have no toys," Dominick explained as he stopped to look at his parents as if they had asked a stupid question. "I be a good sharer," he said.

"Yes, sweetie, you are a good sharer and just for that when we get home Mommy's going to take you to get a bigger Spiderman. Okay?"

"Now, Mommy, I get 'piderman now, peeze."

"Okay, if Daddy wants to take you to get it now, then it's fine with me."

"Come on, little man, let's go get your Spiderman." Jonathan said as he picked up his son with one big swoop of his arm.

Chapter 15

Savannah watched them pull away and she went back to packing. She went into the study where she found all of her mother's journals and decided to take them all. There was a big box of them in the closet that she had not even touched yet, so she decided to definitely take all of them. Now that she would not have to go to work, she could read them. After an hour, she thought she heard a noise in the house. She listened and yes, she heard the back door opening and someone was in the kitchen. Savannah thought the guys must be back and went out to see Dominick's new toy. She put the journals back in the box and taped it up. She walked down the hall and toward the kitchen. She was about to call her husband and son when she got the feeling that something was not right. "*Stay quiet and listen,*" she heard deep down in her spirit. She just stood in the hall, fear creeping up on her. As the noises got louder, she thought about calling Jonathan's cell. Where did she leave her phone? She could not think. Where was her purse? How could she defend herself from some big guy? She prayed. The only thing that came to mind was Jesus having mercy.

In the spiritual realm, Marcus stood directly in front of Savannah with Paul on her right, Fred on her left; Jonas took the position behind her. All were ready to fight for this child of God as she called for help. They stood with fiery swords in hand. All of them stood fifteen feet high dwarfing Savannah. These tall muscular-built angelic beings with piercing eyes stood invisibly protecting her. They knew the danger that lurked just a few feet away. They also knew that the standoff between them and the demon forces would be soon. The enemy was bent on destroying Savannah and her family and they would not stop.

This battle had been going on since the beginning of time and would end only when the Nazarene returned. For centuries Marcus fought against many demons and this time was no different. His charge was to be protective by all cost and he bore the results of the battles through the years everywhere on his frame. Although the angels all had battle scars, they were renewed by the prayers of the children of God and being in the Holy presence of the Almighty.

Marcus knew that currently, he was dealing with two main demons, Anger and Unforgiveness. These two strongholds could only be totally defeated by fasting and prayer. The victim of their attachment became convinced that the thoughts they implanted were her own and after being worked on for so long, the voice that spoke was adopted as well. Once this happened, it took the intercession of someone strong in the faith to overcome the demonic forces and free the victim, which in this case was Rose.

They had attached themselves to Rose and she had given complete control of her mind to them. She was convinced that everyone was against her despite any evidence to the contrary. Currently she was in the kitchen searching for anything she could take to sell for drugs. The nice clothes and designer handbag she came from Chicago with were long gone; she sold them to get high. She managed to scrounge up some clothes from some Christian ministers that passed out food and clothing around the corner from the crack house. She put the clothes on just so she would not be cold but traded the food for one more small hit. With the children out of the way, Rose had spent the few days after the funeral going from marijuana to cocaine then to crack when she ran out of money. She hooked up with a guy from the bus station to simply get a joint. Shortly after the funeral, she found herself snorting cocaine along with others in a back room of the Compound nightclub in downtown Atlanta.

There were plenty of drugs for everyone because of all the celebrities and athletes in the club that night. Rose and her new friend heard one of the celebs say that they were moving the party to his house once the club shut down. So, Rose and her new friend followed the caravan south. They drove to a mansion hidden away in the woods about thirty minutes from Atlanta. For a brief moment, Rose thought about her children, but quickly pushed the thought from her mind as they drove the old dodge down the long driveway to the massive house. After some coaxing, Rose tried the good stuff and was instantly hooked. This cocaine was pure and uncut, the kind that can only be obtained with the right connections. The demons danced around the house with glee. They went from person to person enticing each to do more and more.

Rose sold everything she had to sell including her own body. In a matter of days, she found herself in a house in the heart of Atlanta with a bunch of other people. All of the men had taken several turns with her until they no longer wanted her. She was trash now and the only thing she could do was to give them Tasha. She knew that it was a horrible thing to do, but her sensibilities were gone and, at this point, all she cared about was getting that next hit. The guy she met at the bus station was more than happy to give her another hit. All she needed to do was bring her daughter back to get some more he told her. With the high still fresh in her mind and Tasha gone she needed something to appease the dealer. Rose lied to the man and said that Tasha was gone but would be back later. She begged for a tiny hit and she would bring her later. "No more freebies" he yelled and kicked her out of the car on Cobb Parkway in the heart of Marietta.

Not knowing what to do to get the next hit, Rose wondered around the city thinking thoughts that did not belong to her. The demonic influence of Adonis was strong. *"Go back to Bertha's house and get whatever you can. You deserve to have something. She had all that money and would not help you while she was alive".*

The diatribe went on and on vacillating between hatred of her family, Brian, old boyfriends, babies' daddies, the welfare system, then back to her family again. The blame was placed everywhere except where it belonged. That was the point the demonic forces would shift blame to others so that the target would not do any introspection. They used all kinds of distractions to keep Rose from seeking out and dealing with her real problems.

Bertha had to learn the hard way that she could not help Rose. She had given her so much money over the years. She even paid for rehab after she found out that Rose was pregnant with Tasha. Rose had stayed clean for a while, but the drugs and demons called to her like a lover on a cold night. When Tasha was young Bertha sent money to help with the expenses. Rose gave Bertha a story about how Brian was not working, and they did not have enough money for baby stuff. The thousand dollars she sent was gone in a few days. Even Brian smoked the weed with her. It wasn't until Tasha got really sick that Brian woke up and turned his back on marijuana and liquor a few years later. Eventually Brian began to feel bad when Rose did not return Bertha's calls and she started to call him. He finally confessed to smoking up the money she sent. Bertha was furious and a huge fight ensued that left the sisters not speaking to one another. Anger and Unforgiveness came to inhabit Rose and she welcomed them with open arms. Over the years their hold on her became increasingly stronger as Rose did more and more drugs.

As the noises grew, Savannah continued to ask God for protection and wisdom. "Oh, God, please help me," she said as she crept back into the study to use the phone there. "*Lock the door,*" she heard and did so quietly. She stood there trying to think of her husband's number and her hand shook violently as she dialed the number. Jonathan did not answer so she left a message. Her thinking became frantic. She wondered if she should try to get out the window, but then decided to call the police. Okay, think straight she told herself as she picked the receiver backup to dial 911. As she did, she heard Rose talking to herself and dropped the phone back in its place.

Now angry, Savannah marched back out the study and towards the voice, which was now in the living room.

"What do you think you are doing?" she yelled at her aunt.

Rose swung around quickly. But the initial shock of someone being in the house left just as quickly.

"What do you want?" Savannah barked.

Rose shot back, "I want something to remember my sister by."

"Like what?" Savannah spat back.

"I want some of that money she left you. Bertha left you a lot of money so you say and I want it. She owes me so now you do."

"I'm not giving you a dime. Don't think I don't know that Brian paid for your bus tickets after I sent you all that money to fly here. You are not getting anything else from me. Mama didn't owe you anything and neither do I, so you need to leave here and don't ever come back!"

Ignoring the statement Rose said, "You still have not told me how much."

"And I am not going to either. You need to leave here now before I call the police."

"Whatever, little girl. So, are you going to give it to me or what?"

"Are you deaf or something? I said I'm not giving you anything!" Savannah said with disgust.

"Bertha owed it to me she never helped me out," Rose said as she roamed around the living room opening drawers. "She was always looking down on me because I was not perfect like her. And because I didn't go to church like she did. She thought she was better than me. Your mother was a hypocrite. Aren't Christians supposed to help those in need? I am certainly in need. I got those four kids plus my old man is barely making enough to keep the lights on. The only thing keeping us going is my welfare check and food stamps. So, as I see it, I'm owed something."

Getting tired of the conversation and the venom and hate pouring out of Rose, Savannah shook her head. "Your life is a result of the choices you made. Nobody owes you anything!" she yelled. "I am not going to let you tear up my Mama's house! You need to leave!" She had dropped the thought that Rose was her aunt from her mind. She could not imagine this woman even being related to her mother.

Chapter 16

"What you think you gon do 'bout it if I just take what I want?"

The threat hung in the air. Savannah watched Rose. Her skin color seemed to go from a cappuccino brown to a deep dark chocolate in a matter of seconds. Stunned, Savannah could see what looked like a man in Rose's face. She studied Rose for a second. She could not believe what she was seeing. It was a man's face! Rose squirmed with hatred ready to pounce on Savannah. It was Adonis that brought Anger and Unforgiveness with him to this more than willing vessel. Savannah was speechless watching the face of the principality indwelt within Rose. *What is going on?* she thought. I must be seeing things she told herself as Marcus touched her eyes again.

"Jesus," she whispered as she backed away back down the hall. Slowly Rose walked through the living room towards her knocking over the glass-domed table clock that Savannah had given to her mother for Mother's Day. Heading straight for Savannah, Rose shoved her to the ground and stepped over her. The force of the blow knocked the wind out of Savannah. *How did Rose get so strong?,* she wondered. She felt like she had been hit by a man. She sat on the floor trying to catch her breath then she heard a car pull up into the driveway.

Rose went straight to the ebony jewelry box in Bertha's master bedroom. It was another gift from Savannah. The box had three picture slots on its lid. When Savannah had given it to her mother, she had left two slots empty, but the center 3x5 slot held an old picture of her mother, father and Savannah when she was young. Rose grabbed a handful of jewelry out of it.

"Put that back!" Savannah demanded as she managed to get to her feet and stumble to the bedroom.

"What are you going to do about it, little girl?"

Savannah heard the words but did not see Rose's lips move; she was just glaring at her. Hearing a car door close outside, Savannah sighed with relief because she did not have to deal with Rose alone. Savannah blocked Rose from leaving the room by standing in the doorway of the room. Placing the jewelry in her pocket with one hand Rose knocked Savannah to the floor with the other. Rose stepped over her and she left the room.

"Jonathan!" Savannah screamed, as she got to her knees and pulled herself up. Holding onto the doorknob she quickly stepped over the box she had been packing and peered out the window to see Jonathan getting out of the car and walking around to the other side. *"Good,"* she thought as she picked up the phone and dialed 911. As she talked to the operator, she could hear Rose rummaging through things in another room. She assured the 911 operator that she simply needed the police to come and make Rose leave. Savannah hung up the phone when Jonathan opened the door. She yelled his name again. Hearing the panic in his wife's voice he rushed to the master bedroom. Dominick was so engrossed with his new action figure that he stayed in the living room playing, oblivious to everything.

Reaching the room Jonathan found Savannah out of breath.

"Get her out of here!" she shouted.

"Who?" he asked.

"Rose!" she shouted and turned Jonathan around and walked behind him. There was no time for questions or to tell him what she saw. He wouldn't believe her anyway; she didn't even believe it. "What happened?"

he asked alarmed at the look on Savannah's face.

"She's got Mama's jewelry." "You need to give back the jewelry," he demanded.

"Or what?" Rose sneered and turned her back to them.

"Or I will call the police."

"I already did," Savannah piped in still behind Jonathan.

"Well, I will tell them that you kidnapped my kids," she retorted.

"That is not going to work. You abandoned them. You are the one who will be going to jail," Savannah spat back. Jonathan gave his wife a pat on the arm to say let me handle it.

Marcus stepped back and surveyed the scene ready to protect the family. He has a plan; we can't intervene. As they looked on, Fred and Jonas said in unison, "We will return." God had another assignment for them, and they disappeared. The protector and Spiritual sight stepped into the doorway between the kitchen and living room. Paul touched the little boy as he played. Marcus wrapped his wings around the little one until he was told to let it happen. With that command he released the child.

Dominick walked into the kitchen and looked at Rose. "You a bad bird," he said pointing his little finger at Rose.

Neither Jonathan nor Savannah heard him since they were trying to deal with Rose. But Adonis heard the child and stepped toward him. Before his parents could react, Rose backhanded Dominick, sending him into the wall. He hit his head and slumped to the ground unconscious. In one simultaneous move Savannah rushed to her son while Jonathan swung at Rose. He connected with Rose's face. Rose stepped back and turned her back to Jonathan. Adonis growled. Rose grabbed a knife out of the butcher block on the granite countertop. With one fell swoop, she turned and welded the knife at Jonathan. She cut Jonathan's arm as he tried to pin her down. A crimson stain began to appear on the sleeve of Jonathan's shirt. As Jonathan tried to grab the knife, Rose flipped it in her hand. She lunged at Jonathan and as he stumbled, she sliced again, this time across the chest. Jonathan looked down at his now torn and bloody shirt. The light blue shirt with the silver pin stripes quickly turned a deep shade of red with Jonathan's blood flowing so quickly. "*She is going to kill me*," he thought as he fell. "*I have got to fight. I have to protect my family.*

Lord, give me the strength." He prayed and was able to hold Rose off.

Savannah heard the sirens in the distance and said, "Oh, thank you, Lord!"

Savannah lifted Dominick's little body off the kitchen floor and carried him through the living room. In seconds, she was out the door and with tears rolling down her face. She met the officers pulling into the driveway. "*What if my baby is dead?*" she thought. She tried to listen for his breathing, but she did not hear anything. "*Lord, he can't be dead! God, please! NO!*" She forced herself to calm down as the officers got out of the car.

"Lord, I know You wouldn't do this to me," she cried. "Please, Lord, let my son and husband be okay." She quickly prayed. Both Marcus and Paul began to flap their wings per God's instruction, and the boy stirred in his mother's arms.

"Oh, thank you, Lord!" she said. "Please, God, protect Jonathan," she managed to get out between sobs. In that instant Marcus left them to confront Adonis having been called to action by the prayers she uttered.

The officers barely got to Savannah before she began to gush out the whole story. After they told her to calm down and speak more slowly, she explained the situation to them. One officer left right away at hearing that a weapon was involved. The other officer told Savannah to wait for the ambulance and was just a few steps behind the lead officer. Savannah had to check on Jonathan so, ignoring the police, she cautiously followed them toward the house. The one that spoke to her the first time noticed her and yelled, "Stay here!"

Savannah stood in the doorway sobbing. She heard one of the officers call for backup and an ambulance.

"Police," they called out as they walked through the front door, hands on their holsters. They found Jonathan on the floor with Rose standing over him about to stab him.

They yelled, "Police! Put the knife down now!" as they drew their weapons.

Rose looked up at the officers and screamed, "Fuck you!"

Jonathan lay on the floor, his bloody arms trying to block the blow as Rose bore down on him. Both police shot simultaneously. One, two, three shots rang out in the tiny kitchen.

Savannah rushed into the house, the child still in her arms, screaming, "Jonathan!" Just then another two patrol cars pull up to the house.

"Ma'am, go back outside," ordered one officers in the kitchen as he turned his head to her with the gun still directed at its target.

Savannah ignored him and moved just a little closer to see if her husband was okay.

"How can this be happening? Oh, God . . ." she uttered. Seeing Jonathan's bloody shirt she gasped thinking the police shot him.

"Ma'am," the same officer yelled, "You have to get out of here, now!"

It was not until she saw Jonathan move that she took a breath. She then looked and saw that it was Rose that they shot. Savannah squeezed Dominick tighter to her chest and ran out the front door. More police and an ambulance pulled into the driveway. She rushed to the EMTs and handed Dominick to them.

She watched as they worked on her little boy. She winced as they stuck a needle into his tiny arm. Savannah was never able to stand needles, thus she never took her son for his shots. She left this task to her husband, but now seeing people poking on her son just added to her anxiety. Yes, it was necessary she knew, but she did not like it one bit. To top it all off, it was Rose that had not only hurt her son but her husband as well. The anger in her was only surpassed by her fear. Anger and fear pranced around Savannah speaking softly in her ears. Both of them are going to die. Rose just killed your son and husband.

"Is he okay?" she asked dreading the answer.

The uniformed EMT with an electronic pad ignored the question and asked, "What happened to him?"

Not wanting to explain, Savannah merely said, "He got hit and bumped his head." She then grabbed the shirt of the second EMT working on her son Savannah yelled, "Is he okay?"

Taking a deep breath, he answered, "He is alive, but we won't know how bad his injuries are until we get him to the hospital."

"My husband is bleeding in there," Savannah said pointing to the house. "He needs help too."

"Okay. I will go check out the husband," the first EMT said and followed Savannah to the house.

An officer would not let Savannah back in the house. Her heart ached from the depths of her soul. She let out a guttural moan for her husband and son.

"This is a crime scene," he told her as he held her back. "I cannot let you back in there," he said as he took a step to block her from entering.

A river began to flow from her eyes, and she called her husband's name again.

"Ma'am, let the EMTs take a look at you to make sure you are okay. You can check on the child as well," he said, still blocking the doorway. "We are going to have to ask you some questions, ma'am."

Savannah heard the police officer call on his radio for another ambulance.

Chapter 17

After a long night, Savannah sat exhausted in her husband's hospital room having just come back from Dominick's room where he still lay unconscious. The doctors said that he may be unconscious for a while so Savannah had slipped out to see about Jonathan. How did this happen? She wondered as she sat. She replayed every detail in her mind as she watched Jonathan sleep. Would he be okay? Would Dominick wake up fine? Would he have some kind of brain damage? She posed the questions in a half prayer half accusation to God.

She needed some support, so she thought about calling Estella. "*She will probably think I am calling to say goodbye*," she thought. She did not want to wake the older woman, but she did not want to go through this alone. So, she reached in her purse for her cell phone. She noticed that she had a missed call from a 702 area code that she did not recognize and a voice mail. She saw that she only had a little bit of battery power left so she decided to listen to the message later. She dialed Estella and filled her in on all that transpired. Estella promised to be at the hospital in the morning.

Yes, she knew in the back of her mind both of her boys would be okay, but why was this happening to her? Why had God chosen this moment to throw her life into chaos? Rose had survived the gun shots and was recovering after the surgery a few floors down.

"Now how is that fair?" she said out loud.

"You must learn to forgive," she heard a soft voice say to her spirit.

"No!" she said so loud that Jonathan stirred.

Two yellow eyes peered into the room. Soothing words came to her mind. How in the world are you supposed to forgive her? She tried to kill you and your family. She does not deserve forgiveness. Let her burn in hell! That's where she needs to be for what she did.

"Yeah, that's right!" Savannah said out loud.

Jonathan rolled over and faced Savannah. "Babe, who you talking to?" he asked in a groggy voice.

"Oh, I'm sorry, honey. I didn't mean to wake you up. How are you feeling?"

"I'm okay, just a little sore. How's my boy?"

Not wanting to upset him Savannah answered, "He's going to be fine, the doctors said."

"So, where is he?"

Savannah inhaled a little too long before she said, "He's in the pediatric ward."

"Okay. What are you not telling me?" he queried.

Taking in another long breath and then letting it out slowly, she told her husband about Dominick. "He's still unconscious. The doctors won't know how he is until he wakes up. The MRI showed that he has a concussion and there was some swelling of his brain."

Jonathan was hurting from his injuries and from the news of his son. At the news Jonathan got angry. He could handle someone hurting him but not his family. Jonathan was seething and contemplating the murder of Rose. He said, "if I could just get my hands on her she would be gone." Savannah agreed initially with him but realized he was not sounding like the even natured man she knew. *"Pray for your husband"* Savannah heard in her spirit.

Savannah knew that both of them could not give in to the anger and hatred they were feeling. Her family needed her to be the strong one now. It was time for her to grow up and stand. She had to take what her mom taught her and put it to action. She began to pray in the spirit. The words flowed out of her like a faucet had been turned on. After a while she began to sing in her heavenly tongue.

After praying so much Anger, hatred and fear left her for a better opportunity.

Savannah walked up to the two officers in the hallway and asked, "What is going to happen to her?"

"Based on your statement and the evidence at the scene," the police officer said, "she will be charged with attempted murder and assault." Savannah let out a deep breath that she was unconsciously holding in.

After a total of five days both her boys were ready to get out of the hospital. Estella stood vigil praying in whatever room Savannah wasn't in. They swapped rooms praying for both Jonathan and Dominick each day. Jonathan was given instructions to follow up with his primary care to remove the stitches he had. Fortunately, no major damage was done but he would need to take it easy for the next few weeks and he would have a slight scar they were told by the physician that discharged him.

After Dominick woke up, he told Savannah how he talked to Nannie. "Nannie say she lub me Mommy," Dominick said. "She say for me to be good. I say okay, I be good Nannie and she went with the good birds again."

"I have something for you," Savannah said. She reached in her purse and pulled out his new Spiderman. The boy shouted "my piderman! Tank you Mommy!" He grabbed the toy from his mom's hand and hugged it.

With some additional instructions the two were released from the hospital. Rose was transferred to jail after she recovered from her gunshot wounds. One of the officers told Savannah and Jonathan that they would need to return for the trial in a few months.

Chapter 18

Movers came and packed up all that Savannah wanted to take back home. They loaded it on a truck and set out for Las Vegas. After saying their goodbyes to Estella and Raul they got on the plane to go back home finally. Atlanta would never be the same place for her she thought looking out the window of the plane.

Savannah looked at her son in the seat between her and Jonathan, then at her husband. So much had happened in such a short period of time. She made it through the fire and came out on the other side stronger, she thought. Yes, she was indeed stronger. She had lost her mom, but she still had her husband and son. "Lord, thank you," she prayed. Then she heard, *"Read the letter,"*

Taking the letter from her purse she opened it and began to read.

"Dear Savannah,

I wish I could be with you to tell you this in person, but God is calling me to be with Him. Puddin', I want you to know more than anything that your father and

I both love you very much and I know you have a lot of questions right now. You may even be mad at me for not telling you all that you are about to find out. Believe me; I wanted to tell you so many times. But I prayed to God and was assured that you had your own mountains you had to climb, but that you would be fine. Your father did not want you to know about the money until you were older and settled. That is why he put in his will to keep the money from you until you were twenty-five. He and I both wanted you to make it on your own first then you would be able to appreciate what we have given you and use it wisely.

As I am writing this, I think about what a beautiful woman you are and how privileged I have been by being your mother. You have turned out to be a wonderful young woman and I know you will do great things. I want you to live blessed, but I also want you to bless others. For God's children, money is to be used for the building up of His kingdom. I have tried to do this with my life and the money your father left me. I hope you do the same. Live your life and enjoy your family because they are the true treasures. Kiss my grandbaby and tell him that I love him. He truly is the joy in my life.

I never told you before, but I am telling you now so that you can be aware. I thought I would have more time to explain everything to you, but it was not His will. There are things you need to know about me and the gift God gave me as a young girl. I have the gift of spiritual sight. I think you know what I mean. I see angels and demons. I think you may have that same gift. I told very few people because most would not have believed. I found this out the hard way.

I remember seeing a man when I was maybe ten or so. He looked like he was from India or somewhere in the Middle East. At first, I thought I was dreaming, but in fact, I was awake. He did not talk to me, but I would talk to him. I called him Marcus. He would always stand in front of me protecting me from a demon that followed me everywhere. Over the years, I prayed and asked God what this demon was doing, and He told me his name was Adonis, and he was assigned to me. His task was to keep me from fulfilling my destiny by killing me, or at the very least, keeping me subdued. At ten years old, I was not thinking about destiny. I was thinking about boys!

Anyway, Adonis was this very scary looking white guy with dreadlocks. Later, when I saw the movie, The Matrix, the albino twins reminded me of what he looked like, except he looked more evil. I knew he would kill me in an instant if it were not for Marcus. He almost succeeded several times. Remember when I told you about being stuck under an eighteen-wheel tractor-trailer? Well that was one of the times. Adonis made the front tire blow out and I ended up between the wheels under the trailer. Marcus stopped the car from going all the way underneath and killing me. I walked away from that accident without a scratch. I am telling you this so that you realize that the spiritual realm is very real.

As I was growing up when different circumstances came up in my life, Adonis would attack and Marcus would protect me. When I was at the age of fourteen, he was joined by another angel I named Jonas. This angel was a white man with very soft features. When I saw him, I really felt encouraged so that is what I called him — Jonas, the Encourager. He was always on my left. It was like he was there to remind me of who I was . . . God's daughter!

Then there was the angel that came to stay when I was sixteen years old. I was really messed up back then. I did not want anything to do with God or church. I was thinking about killing myself. I talked about it for a while, and then I decided that the next day, I was going to do it. That night I went to sleep and suddenly, my eyes popped open and this dark figure was standing by my bed. He was darker than anything else in the room. I tried to scream, but nothing came out. I also tried to move, but I was paralyzed. I heard this very loud voice say, "Do you really want to die?" I was so terrified that I could not even respond. The next thing I knew, it was morning and a new angel had joined Marcus and Jonas, and was standing on my right. When he came, I began to see more and more things in the spirit. I could see that not only was Adonis there trying to kill me, but also there was another demon that would vomit and defecate on me. When this happened, it left me feeling depressed.

This new angel reminded me of an Israeli. He had dark hair and eyes and his clothes were like he was straight out of biblical times. That is why I thought of Paul in the New Testament, so I call him Paul, Spiritual Sight. Still a little lost and not knowing what I was supposed to do, I just went through life with no real purpose. It was not until my twenties that I really began to find my place in God and my purpose in His kingdom. I was passionate about doing what God had created me for.
It was then that Fred came. Now I don't know if these are their real names but it's the names I gave them. Fred, Speak the Truth, is the angel that prompted me to always tell the truth in difficult

situations when no one else will say what needs to be said. He looked like a black man with thick lips and a bald head. He showed up at church one day. I was listening to Pastor Jay. I will never forget, the pastor said something about speaking the truth. This angel appeared right beside him and looked straight at me. He pointed a sword at me, and I heard, "Speak!" His mouth did not move, but I knew it was him speaking. I was stunned and could not take my eyes off him for the whole service. So, he became Fred, Speak the Truth.

I really am sorry that I did not tell you all of this before when we could have had the time to talk about it. In fact, I planned to tell you this Christmas. When I came to your house the last time, I saw a demon outside of your house. When I saw him, I prayed for you that entire visit that God would send His protection like He has for me. I felt at peace. God assured me that the demon could not harm you.

Savannah, please seek God for what He wants you to do with the money you will

be given. It is my wish for you to prosper, but I already know that you have. I just look at my Dominick and I know that God is with you. Again, always know that I love you with all that I have in me. Always remember who you are, Savannah. God has given you so many gifts and you are to use them for His glory.
Mama"

After reading her mother's last words to her, Savannah dissolved into tears. She suddenly realized how great her parents were and how much they loved her. Savannah finally felt peace grip her heart. Her mother and father, she realized, had done everything to protect her and prepare her for this moment. She knew, now, that had she not worked so hard to graduate from college, she wouldn't have appreciated her hard-earned degree. She remembered how good it felt buying their home. They had done it on their own. God had been preparing her, all her life, for this moment! Knowing the path that her life would take; she dried her eyes.

Chapter 19

Jonathan brought the suitcases in from the car and started to take them upstairs. "Babe, the bags can wait. Let's just relax here all together," she said. He came and plopped down next to her. Dominick was already quickly falling asleep in his mother's lap.

"Do you want me to take him and put him to bed," he asked.

"No, I just want you two to be near me right now." So, Jonathan pulled the blanket off the corner of the couch and they fell asleep in each other's arms.

Savannah cooked her boys a hearty breakfast of bacon, eggs and pancakes. They ate and began their normal routine. Jonathan put the suitcases upstairs. When he came back down, he said, "I'm going to take Dominick to school, ok?"

"Yes, that's fine." Savannah said.

"Come on big boy. Let's get ready for school."

"Okay daddy," Dominick said with syrup all over his hands and face. An hour later she kissed them both and they were out the door. She realized that she needed to call Estella and let her know they made it back ok. After a few minutes with the older woman she excused herself because her phone was beeping that another call was coming in.

"Hello, Mrs. Miller. This is Mr. Sewell in human resources. We need you to come in as soon as you get back in town."

"I am back. I can be there in an hour," she said.

"Alright. I'll see you in an hour thanks."

Savannah thought about calling Jonathan, but she decided she could handle it herself. She walked into the building a little early and went to her desk and took all of her personal things and put them in the box she got from the copy room and put it under her desk. She didn't see anyone on the floor yet, which was great because she really didn't want to talk to anyone. Her only real true friend was Jean and she would talk to her outside of this place. She made her way to the third floor where HR was located and walked in. She told the receptionist who she was and who she was to see. The receptionist directed her to the office and Savannah knocked. The door opened and Savannah stood looking at the face of her supervisor Robert King

"Please have a seat Mrs. Miller," said an elderly white man from the leather chair behind a desk. "I asked you to come in because of the disturbing exchange you had with your supervisor. I wanted to bring Mr. King in as well to counsel you as to your behavior. To be honest with you, Mrs. Miller, your conduct was reprehensible and in a normal case you would have been terminated. However, Mr. King informed me that you were under duress with the illness of your mother."

Savannah zoned out for a moment but heard him say demotion and probation. She must have had a strange look on her face because Mr. Sewell said "Do you understand what I am saying to you, Mrs. Miller?"

Savannah thought about all that she had just been through. She thought about how many times she imagined what it would feel like to quit her job. She imagined telling Robert King off. This was her moment. She said "Yes, I understand what you are saying".

He continued, "I also think an apology is in order for Mr. King."

At those words Savannah stood and said, "I understand, but I don't think I am right for this job." She reached in her purse and took her badge out and laid it on Mr. Sewell's desk, turned and walked out of the office.

Savannah got on the elevator feeling great! All the things she was going to say to Robert didn't matter anymore. None of the heartache she endured at his hands mattered;

she was free! Savannah stopped and spoke to a few people that she was friends with and told them it was her last day. Then she saw Robert get off the elevator with Mr. Sewell. Savannah picked up her box, told Jean she would call her and walked right by Robert and Mr. Sewell out the door without another word.

Chapter 20

The weeks became months and the pain of her loss lessened.
Savannah began to see a strength she didn't know she had. She began to find a new normal. The pain of the loss of her mother never left, but she was able to come to terms with it. Now with time on their hands and finances no longer a concern, Jonathan and Savannah began exploring new adventures. Jonathan purchased the garage where he worked. Within months the shop had tripled its business. He needed help so he enlisted Uncle Terrell to come help run it with him.

Savannah decided that she would just stay home and volunteer at Dominick's school once a week. They made the trip back to Atlanta for Rose's trial. When she saw her aunt again, she looked completely different. After testifying she received a written request from Rose for Savannah to come and see her. Savannah braced herself for what would happen seeing the woman that nearly killed her husband and son. Jonathan encouraged her to go.

Savannah walked into the room. It looked just like the TV shows. The room was sterile with a bank of phones, chairs, and a glass divider that split the room. Savannah saw an officer on the other side of the glass standing by the door. After she picked up the nearest phone, she sat down. A moment later, Rose shuffled in. The guard unlocked the chains that bound her, and Rose walked to the phone. Rose looked nothing like she did the last time Savannah saw her. Rose's face was brighter and other than dark circles around her eyes and a missing front tooth, she looked good.

Savannah picked up the phone. "Hey Savannah," Rose said princely. "I didn't think you would come. Well, let me say first that I am so sorry for everything I did to you and your family. I was really messed up. I know that ain't no excuse, but I just wanted to tell you that wasn't me."

"Okay" was all Savannah could say.

"I wanted to say that and to let you know that I'm getting myself together in here. There is a lady that comes every Sunday and teaches about the Bible. I am listening and I am trying to get right with God. I know I am going to be here awhile. I don't know how long yet, but I just wanted to say that I am sorry, and I wanted to know if you could forgive me. I gave my life to God the other day. I prayed that I could get a chance to talk to you and tell you how sorry I am. I want to talk to my kids too, but they prolly won't want to talk to me." Rose paused and just looked at Savannah.

Savannah looked at her aunt and told her "Of course I forgive you. I will be praying for you."

"Thank you," Rose said with tears in her eyes. "That is all that I wanted. Please tell your husband and baby I'm sorry too." Rose said blinking back tears.

"I will tell him what you said." Savannah told her.

"Oh yeah, could you tell Brian I would like to see the kids, if that is possible? I think I will be sent to a prison in Michigan that's not that far from Chicago," She asked.

"I will let him know," Savannah said. The officer by the door said something Savannah couldn't hear and Rose said, "I got to go".

"Okay bye. I'll be praying for you," Savannah said.

"Thanks," Rose replied and hung the phone up.

Back at home they got back into a comfortable groove. Savannah realized that forgiving her aunt was freeing. She truly felt sorry for Rose, but grateful that she had gotten closer to God. She included Rose in her nightly prayer along with Brian, his wife and the children. She told Brian what Rose asked for and he assured her that he would make it happen. He reminded Savannah of their conversation at the arcade and how prayer really did work.

After a grocery store run one day, Savannah got Dominick out of the car and put him on the driveway to walk into the house. "No, Mommy, no! Bad birds get me!" he screamed, and tried to hide behind her legs.

"What birds, baby?" she asked, trying to calm him.

"Birds there. There," he said pointing to the trees.

Savannah looked where Dominick was pointing. Savannah couldn't see anything but in the dark shadows, but two yellow eyes glared back at them.

The End

4HG BOOKS OUR STORY:

4-HG (For His Glory) Books was birthed in 2020 during the global pandemic when everything was shut down. During that downtime God impressed upon Alisha Davis to publish her stories. Not finding a traditional publishing house that would accept her offerings she started 4HG books. Books that had previously sat on the shelf for 10 years now had a home. 4HG Books not only published her own stories but also helps other rejected authors as well. 4HG books distributes Christian fiction and children's literature that highlights diversity and cultural sensitivity.